ROUGHNECKS

Thomas Cochran

ROUGHNECKS

Gulliver Books

Harcourt Brace & Company

San Diego   New York   London

Author's Note

The state of Louisiana has a rich high school football tradition, but I have made no attempt to portray its actual classification or playoff systems here. Oil Camp and Pineview do not exist. All of the other towns that are mentioned do, as does Claiborne Parish; their use is, of course, strictly imaginary.

I would like to acknowledge the encouragement and advice I received from the late Otto Salassi during the earliest stage of this book's composition. He knew the project only as a sketch, but his generosity was such that he took it seriously and believed in it even then, which was an inspiration.

My gratitude for the help of Anne Davies, who seemed always to have the right suggestion at the right time, is complete. Thanks also are due Don and Kim Harington for helping me find my way when I thought I was lost for good.

Library of Congress Cataloging-in-Publication Data
Cochran, Thomas, 1955–
    Roughnecks/Thomas Cochran.
       p. cm.
    "Gulliver Books."
    Summary: Travis Cody prepares for the final game of his high school football career, a rematch with his school's chief rival.
    ISBN 0-15-201433-0
    [1. Football—Fiction.]   I. Title.
PZ7.C6396Ro   1997
[Fic]—dc20   96-43939

Text set in New Baskerville
Designed by G. B. D. Smith
First edition
F E D C B A
Printed in the United States of America

For Debby and Amos

MORNING

1

The house is dark and still when I wake up. I glance at the thin red digits of my clock radio to see how far ahead of the alarm I am. Half an hour. If this were any other day I'd smile, roll over, and return to dreamland. I'd never make it back there today though, so I don't even try. Instead, I reach across and turn the radio on. Creedence Clearwater Revival is raving along near the end of an old number that I like called "Hey Tonight." I make a deal with myself to rise and shine as soon as it's all the way over.

I don't come through. I'm way too warm and my back hardly even hurts. It will as soon as I get up, but right now I'm almost comfortable. The Shreveport DJ, "Mighty" Mike Michaels, lets me know that the temperature is twenty-eight degrees and that we're looking at another clear-as-a-bell Jim Dandy here in the Ark-La-Tex. We can expect a high today in the midfifties and a low tonight of around thirty. Sounds like football weather to me.

I click Mighty Mike off, switch on my lamp, and

swing my legs over the side of the bed. When my feet touch the cold tile I shiver. Then—three, two, one, *zero*—I stand and take a deep breath. Exhaling slowly I bend to test my back. I reach for my toes but there's no way. The muscles beg for mercy. They feel like they're nailed to boards. I can hardly get my fingertips to my ankles. It's just pain though, so I can take it. I can even play with it. It's not at all like last year when I wrecked my elbow. That was pure injury. PAIN AND INJURY. One of the signs in our training room says that we're supposed to know the difference between the two and I do. It's large. There's no mistaking the place where the first leaves off and the second begins.

I move to my window. Resting my chin on the heels of my hands, I gaze out but the light from the lamp hits the glass so that all I can see is the reflection of my face. I cut the lamp off then I look back out the window. The sky is still black but my eyes begin to adjust and soon I can make out the tree line of the woods behind the neighboring houses. A gentle breeze is nudging the tops of the tallest pines, causing them to sway like slow dancers. A few stars remain visible but the moon is gone and the sun is on its way. The most important day of my life is about to dawn.

It's that simple. This is the most important day of my life so far. I've had some important ones in the past, but those were different because the things that made them important happened unexpectedly, in the normal way. There's nothing unexpected about this one. What's going to happen is scheduled. My final game as an Oil Camp Roughneck is on the agenda, a college coach is going to be watching me, and I'll be working against Jericho Grooms again, which is like having a prayer answered.

We got the good word shortly after beating South Cameron in the semis last Friday. Coach Crews had just delivered a postgame address about how winning is one of life's great pleasures and about how celebrating it is fine as long as you realize that past accomplishments don't amount to much when you've got another game coming up. Our business, he said, wasn't quite finished. Pure Crews. He's a firm believer in focus and perspective. He insists on them at all times. If you had walked in there without knowing what was going on, you would never possibly have guessed that we'd just won a semifinal playoff game against the second-ranked club in the state—on the road, in the rain—by nineteen points. But that's part of Crews's method. He keeps us hungry by tossing us only scraps of praise and he's stingy even with those. We know we can't entirely please him, but like all of his teams we've won a bunch of games trying to.

After he wrapped up his speech he kneeled down and led us through our traditional recital of the Lord's Prayer. Then he stood, held up a hand, and worked his jaw muscles.

"One more thing, men," he said.

We were gathered around him like disciples, which in a way I suppose we are, each of us on a knee in our grimy uniforms. He paused and studied the floor, tracing and retracing an invisible line on the concrete with the toe of his right shoe. It was an intense moment. All you could hear was the sound of a running urinal and an occasional sniff. Several proud daddies and older brothers were in there with us and while we waited for Crews to tell us what we hoped we already knew, I looked around and wished that my brother, Glen, had been able to make the trip instead of having to work. It would have been nice to share this with him.

I needed to stand and stretch because my back was starting to tighten but I couldn't until Crews was done so I shifted into a sitting position, rested my forehead on my knees, and stared at my high-tops. They were muddy, coated with grass, and taped at the ankles for extra support and to keep the laces secure. I whispered the word *please* to myself.

Finally Crews spoke.

"I have you a final from up home," he said.

I lifted my head. Crews was as close to smiling as he ever lets himself get and I knew for sure what was coming.

"It's Pineview," he said.

There was a heartbeat of absolute silence before we went ape. We sprang to our feet and whooped. We acted like rescued castaways. We hugged and fived. We danced and chanted.

"Rematch! Rematch! Rematch!"

We strolled around fast-clapping our hands and repeating the word over and over until it dissolved in a wave of caveman hollering. All of us had been pulling hard for Pineview throughout the playoffs. It wasn't easy but it had to be done. Now we could resume hating their guts again like normal and it was a great feeling. The Pelicans were coming to our place for the state championship.

When I got to the house after the long bus ride home, Glen was there. It was late but he had dropped by and was waiting for me in the den with the TV going. An incredibly good-looking woman was gliding around in her underwear on HBO. I sat down and admired the way she carried herself. Glen ignored me at first because he was enjoying the scene too. Then it changed to some men shooting pool in a bar. Glen held out the remote, zapped the movie, and stared at the blank screen.

"Well, we did it," I said. "In case you didn't hear."

Glen nodded, still not looking at me.

"I heard," he said. "I also heard that Pineview did it too and that's why I'm over here. I want to tell you something."

"I'm listening," I said.

"Not too many people ever get a second chance in this life, boss. I just hope you appreciate the fact that you've gotten yourself one."

"You sound exactly like Pawpaw," I said.

"I said I hope you appreciate the fact that you just got yourself a second chance, brother."

"I appreciate it," I said. "Brother."

He turned to face me and we looked each other straight in the eye for a few seconds.

"Good," he said. "You deserve it."

"Thanks, Glen," I said.

"No need to thank me," he said.

"Yeah, there is," I said. "I wasn't sure what you been thinking lately."

"Well, Travis, what I've been thinking lately is that I'm real damn proud of you for hanging in there," he said. "OK?"

Glen's the kind of guy who is uncomfortable expressing anything that resembles an emotion. I could see that he was embarrassed. What he'd said was plenty though. It meant a lot to me because it was the first time that he'd acknowledged what I've been going through for the past month. I've played some pretty good ball during the playoffs, but people around here have long memories so he'd undoubtedly heard some trash directed my way.

"OK," I said.

"Tell me about the game," Glen said.

I knew that he'd probably listened to bits and pieces of it on the radio, but I started from the beginning and filled him in on the parts he'd missed, including the safety South Cameron scored in the fourth period when my buddy Lunk backed into me and blocked one of my punts. Glen shook his head.

"I predict a little extra work after practice for the Lunker come Monday," he said.

"Yep," I said. "He'll pay."

I didn't know it yet but I was going to catch some flak about that play myself—not because I'd done anything wrong but because of the way it was written up, completely wrong, in the Shreveport paper's game report the next day.

Before he left, Glen punched me on the arm and repeated what he'd said about second chances.

"Keep it in mind," he said.

"Don't worry," I said.

"This is it, little bro."

Still watching the pines I think: A few hours from now it really will be. A few hours from now we'll be on the field and then I'll have forty-eight minutes to redeem myself for making the mistake that cost us an undefeated regular season. Sometimes things work out the way you hope they will. Once in a while you get what you want and for me this is one of those times. I've spent the past month wanting another shot at Jericho Grooms and the Pineview Pelicans as badly as I've ever wanted anything in my life.

2

Jericho Grooms is the best lineman in our district and one of the best in the state, a bona fide blue-chipper whose daddy just happened to get transferred from east Texas to northwest Louisiana last summer. I first heard of him the Sunday the Shreveport paper's preseason tabloid came out. There was a feature story about him in it and he has been on my mind almost constantly ever since.

I press my forehead against the window. The glass is so cold that I can feel it all the way down into my jaw. I don't move away because it's a nice sensation. It fits with the darkness and the silence of my room. A moment later I hear a truck that doesn't have a muffler pass in front of the house. Somebody's starting early or finishing late. The noise gradually fades until it's no longer audible and I realize that I've begun to bump the glass with my forehead. I'm not doing it hard, just steadily. Tonight Grooms and I will be bumping our heads together as hard as we can.

The preseason tab is at the bottom of a pile of

stuff over on my desk. I haven't pulled it out for a while but I know exactly where it is and I can quote the opening paragraph of the feature on Grooms:

> He has size and speed and an unlisted telephone number. The football gods blessed him with the first two, and college scouts drove him to the third. Now he's living in a different area code, but the scouts know his new address. They know that Jericho Grooms, late of Lufkin, Texas, has taken up residence in Pineview, giving the already loaded Pelicans an extra boost in the race for this year's District 1AA championship and making coach Charlie Webb's club a serious contender for the Class AA state crown.

When I read that back in August I figured the guy for a fullback or a tight end on offense and a linebacker on defense, but later on in the article it said that Webb planned to play him up front and in the middle both ways, center on O and noseguard on D. This meant that when we met Pineview I'd have him one-on-one all night, which I did.

That was on November 20, in our regular season finale. Except when I punted, Grooms was directly across from me and he was every bit the stallion that had been advertised. He was relentless. He never let up, never coasted. Most guys will take a play or two off at some point but Grooms was the real, 100-percent-of-the-time deal. He just kept coming and he seemed to get stronger as the game went on. It was amazing. I've had to dig deep before but I had to go to an unknown level just to stay with this monster, especially late. He was at his best late.

For the next few days most of the people I saw told me that I did a great job against him, but I suspected that they were only trying to make me feel better about what happened at the end. I figured that in spite of their kind words they had to have been thinking the same thing the son of a bitch who has called me on the telephone several times since then comes right out and says: *"You blew it, Cody. You choked, Cody. You cost us that game, Cody."*

All I ever get to say to him is, "Who is this?" He never answers though. He just says what he has to say and hangs up. I haven't heard from him since Monday, but every time I answer the phone I half expect it to be him calling to hassle me some more. I don't know what the guy thinks he's accomplishing. Maybe he thinks he's doing me a favor, inspiring me to try harder or something. If so, he's mistaken. All he's doing is making me realize how out of hand people in this town can get about football, myself included. Sometimes I wish I'd been born in a place where nobody had ever even heard of it.

Football is such a big deal in Oil Camp that when you're born here you get a miniature plastic ball from the Touchdown Club if you're a boy. This is practically the first thing that happens in your whole life. You get a football that's black with gold stripes and lettering. The lettering reads: ANOTHER ROUGHNECK. That may or may not turn out to be the case but the pressure is on and the message is clear: "Oil Camp is football country, son, and you need to understand that up front. There's only one game that matters in your hometown. Believe this. Believe also that the time will come when you'll need to decide whether you're going to buy in and be a part of it or not, so here's a little something to help you start making up your mind. Look it over good. Hold it in your hands. Get used to it."

You've been in the world for less than thirty minutes and you already own a football. It's a bizarre thing when you really think about it, but nobody objects because it's an old custom with deep roots and as long as there's an Oil Camp, it's not going to change because football is king here. People are obsessed with it.

I was one of those who bought in early. I loved the feel of the ball even before my hands were big enough to hold one that was regulation size. I loved the leather smell and the strange shape of it. I loved passing and catching and kicking it. I even loved the unpredictable way it bounced when it hit the ground. Later I fell in love with the game itself. First there's touch, then there's flag, then there's tackle. I loved them all. I loved the progressively faster and more violent swirl of motion. I loved getting up on Saturday mornings, dressing out in the New Orleans Saints replica uniform that was all I wanted for Christmas when I was in the fifth grade, and spending the entire day slamming into my friends on the elementary school playground. I loved pretending that I was a football player.

Eventually I learned that the game isn't about pretending though. It's about being who and what you are without illusions. It's about lining up against somebody and finding out who can and who can't, who's a winner and who's a loser. You get to fake it for a while, but the time comes when you have to put away your toy uniform, strap on a real one, and start facing the truth about yourself while the whole town watches you and judges every move you make. Buy in and if you don't get anything else for your trouble, you'll surely get that. It's not always easy to deal with the truth about yourself either.

The fact of the matter is that I did handle Grooms reasonably well most of the time the other night. But most of the time wasn't good enough because he wasted me in the crunch. He lunched me when it counted. He caused me to miss my assignment on the single most crucial play of the season and the result was that his team won and my team lost. I don't need anybody to remind me of that. Still, it wasn't like I was the only one out there. And it wasn't like I let Grooms get past me on purpose. The problem is that I didn't finish the play the way I should have. I didn't go down fighting. If I had, I wouldn't care what anybody thought. I pulled a muscle in my back trying to stop him, but that's just a detail, not an excuse, and it doesn't change anything. It doesn't allow me to doubt myself any less. Grooms forced me to give up before the play was over, something I've never done. He made me quit and I've been haunted by that memory because I can't stand to think of myself as a quitter.

Regardless of how you look at it, the bottom line is that because I got my butt whipped, Pineview got the district title and we got to watch them celebrate. It was sickening. Losing to anybody would have been bad enough, but I'm pretty sure that even the nut who keeps calling me on the telephone wouldn't be so upset if it had been Plain Dealing or Cotton Valley that beat us. I'm also pretty sure that in that case I wouldn't feel quite as horrible about it as I do. But Pineview is only twelve miles from here and our game with them is the biggest thing that happens in either town every year. The rest of what goes on doesn't mean anything, compared.

We call Pineview South Oil Camp but that has never been anything more than wishful thinking on our part, and these days it's just plain idiotic because they were better prepared for the oil bust than we were. They have a Wal-Mart, a Hardee's, and a lake people from all over the region drive to for fishing, skiing, and camping. They also have a newly restored turn-of-the-century courthouse that stands on a magnolia-lined lawn in the middle of an active downtown square. Pineview is a pretty town, which nobody ever accused Oil Camp of being. We have two things they don't have down in the parish seat though. One is a collection of state championship trophies in our case. The other is a winning record in the Pineview–Oil Camp series. We've beaten them more often than they've beaten us through the years, and they're just as aware of that as we are because they have a pretty strong football tradition themselves. It's just not as strong as ours. When people talk Louisiana high school football history, they'll mention Pineview but they'll dwell at length on Oil Camp. We like to keep this in mind whenever we go down there. We're always a factor in our class.

The sportswriters liked Pineview this year though,

primarily because of Grooms. We had a couple of question marks going in, but we answered those early and it was clear that we were shaping up as the best Oil Camp team since Glen's undefeated junior season when the Roughnecks took state for the last time. The atmosphere around here for nine straight weeks was like a carnival. We were winning big and moving steadily up in the Class AA poll after opening at number eight. The timing couldn't have been better because the bust had really started taking its toll on the town. Oil Camp was struggling, but that didn't seem to matter quite as much because the Roughnecks were doing their thing. People were comparing us to the great teams of the past and every Friday night we took them away from their problems for a little while. We gave them something to believe in, something to be proud of. No team we played on the road had more fans in the stands than we did and most didn't have as many. We were red-hot, unbeaten, and ranked third—behind Pineview and South Cameron—entering the final week of the regular season. Then, just like *that,* it was all over. Our success in the playoffs has bandaged the wound, but it's still there and it still hurts.

I practiced like a sick dog on the Monday after we lost and even worse the following afternoon. We were trying to learn a new game plan and I couldn't concentrate on it. My back bothered me some but the main trouble was that I was distracted. I had too much on my mind to focus on what I was supposed to be doing and I wasn't even sure that I wanted to be doing it anymore. I kept thinking about just saying the hell with it and walking off the field, which made me feel even more worthless than I already did.

Crews noticed, of course.

"You've got to let it go, son," he said after our Tuesday wind sprints. "It's done. Put it behind you."

"Yessir," I said.

There's a sign tacked to the back side of our dressing room door that reads SACRIFICE—one black word on a square of white poster paper. We're supposed to touch it every time we go through the door and I've always done this without thinking much about it. Standing in the shower that evening I started thinking about sacrifice real hard. I was in there by myself and as the hot water came down on me, I remembered how much I'd sacrificed to be a Roughneck. I thought about being so weary and hurt that I couldn't focus my eyes. I thought about pulling muscles, breaking bones, and pissing blood. I thought about all the exhausting trips up and down the bleachers at Roughneck Field, all the blinding collisions in Blood Alley, all the disorienting sessions of Bull in the Ring.

It seemed like I hadn't done much of anything else *but* sacrifice during the past three years. Once I got on it the cycle never stopped: Fourth Quarter weight training. Spring Ball. Summer Conditioning. Preseason two-a-days. The season itself. Start over. Do it again. It had been a long, painful haul. I still loved the game but I could feel myself beginning to cave in under the weight of what I'd gone through to play it. I'd sacrificed, all right. And for what? I didn't have an answer.

Standing there I realized it was nearly over. We were down to at most four more weeks and if we made it that far we'd surely meet Pineview again because they were in the opposite bracket. The key word was *we*. I reminded myself of the lesson Crews had tried to teach me during Spring Ball last April, when I came back from the elbow injury that ended my junior season early. The lesson was that I was part of a bigger thing. I was a member of a team. I was a Roughneck. Remembering this allowed me to take a small step toward understanding the point of the sacrifices I'd made, pulling myself together, and rejoining the cause.

After supper that night I went to my room and found the date of the state finals on my Harley-Davidson calendar. I stared at it for a while then I wrote *Pineview vs. Oil Camp* inside the square with a red marker. I looked to the future in order to live with the past and get on with the present. It was simplistic but it was also optimistic and it helped. I was feeling better before the ink dried. I had a definite goal: to finish what I'd started the day I was born and the doctor or the nurse or whoever it was put that little football with ANOTHER ROUGHNECK stamped on it into my crib.

Now I'm down to the final task and I'll have a good idea of how well I'll complete it after our first offensive play. Like the rest of the team I'm putting some extra chips on that one. We're passing, which we rarely do at all and never do early. Pineview will freak—or so we hope. We're counting on them to read run because that's how we block it. Inside Belly Pass. Grooms will attack and I plan to meet him with everything I have because I want him on the ground. I won't be satisfied with anything less. It has to be a pancake. I know it's a chancy move to think that way but I need to own him on that first play so I can quit doubting myself. You can't be successful against a player like Jericho Grooms if you have any doubts whatsoever. He'll feed on them and break you and then it's all over, for you and for your team.

3

Having to play on Saturday has thrown me. I've got things I always do on a game day, but Friday is our normal game day and it's a school day. Saturday is a workday, totally different. It seems crazy to me that after thirteen Friday games the Athletic Association makes the finalists in every classification wait an extra day to play the most important games of the season. I'm not into it. I have my rituals and this confuses them. Thanks to the scheduling Einsteins down in Baton Rouge, everything I do this morning has the potential to be wrong. I bet Grooms isn't having this kind of trouble with his day. I bet he's fast asleep and dreaming about taking me apart.

Humming the Creedence tune I heard earlier, I slide open the door to my closet and rummage through the dirty clothes basket in search of my double-cotton turtleneck. It used to be Pawpaw's. Mom has been after me to throw it into the rag bag and get a new one but that's because she doesn't understand charms. This one is playoff proven.

The temperature was in the low twenties the Friday after Thanksgiving when we played Oak Grove in the first round. I had some trouble with my rituals that morning too because we were out of school for the holiday, but the game was on the road and I have another set of procedures to cover that. We left fairly early anyway so I was back on track before I'd done any serious damage. Because it was going to be so cold that night I wanted to wear something under my jersey during the game. I found a box of winter stuff in the attic and sorted through it. I wasn't looking for anything in particular but when I found the double-cotton I knew I had what I wanted. I pulled it out, held it up to my face, and breathed in the smell of it. Pawpaw. His mixture of Vitalis and Old Spice and Captain Black pipe smoke was still there. It was probably as much imaginary as real but it made me feel strong. I wore the shirt in the game that night and because we won I've worn it every Friday since, including yesterday. Even though I forgot to wash it last night, I wouldn't walk out of the house this morning without having it on for all the wells in the world.

The rest of my outfit for the day includes my lucky jeans, my lucky tube socks, and my lucky Chuck Taylor All Stars. I carry the pile across the hall to the bathroom. My jersey is at the stadium. Crews had us turn them in after yesterday's walk-through. We're supposed to pick them up and wear them to the pep rally this afternoon. I'm a little uneasy about not having mine here but there's nothing I can do about that. Surely the Fates will understand.

I take a long leak and dress, then I inspect my face

in the medicine cabinet mirror above the sink. I don't get that many places but when I do they're always the kind that take forever to heal. One of them has been going through the preliminaries since Tuesday. It's just below the right corner of my mouth, a favorite hangout among pimples I have known. I thought I might be able to start working on it in earnest today but it's still in the red blotch stage so I decide to leave it alone. A plain zit is bad enough. One with a bruise around it looks like disease.

Dabbing some Sea Breeze on the red spot, I check out my hair, which is looking OK this morning. I used to wear it a lot longer than I do now but I got tired of constantly having to fool with it. I even had a ponytail for a while in junior high. Pawpaw gave me endless hell about that experiment. He'd say that he'd never seen a male of the species who worried about his hairdo as much as his younger grandson. I'd tell him that he was just jealous because he didn't have enough hair left to worry about. These days all I have to do is put a little water on it, brush it straight back, and let it do whatever it wants to. Pawpaw would be proud to know that I've simplified.

My standard game-day breakfast is a chocolate shake and two pieces of oven toast painted with Mom's blue-ribbon preserves, strawberry or peach depending on supply and mood. Pawpaw called it sissy food. His idea of breakfast was the recipe he published in the *Touchdown Club Cookbook* a few years ago. It's a fine meal but there's no way I could hold it down on the day of a game. Listen to this:

JOE CODY SR.'S GUT-CHECK OMELETTE

4 eggs, beaten
1 jalapeño, sliced
1 garlic clove, crushed
½ white onion, minced
1 tomato, cut into bits

Stir ingredients together in a skillet over medium heat until done, smother with black pepper, and serve with blood sausage, cathead biscuits, and sorghum molasses.

Maybe I'll square off against one of those tomorrow. Today it would only lead to regret.

I open the oven. Mom fixed some toast before she left for work at the hospital. She's a nurse and she's on the early shift this weekend. I stick a couple of slices in the microwave then gather the items I need for my shake. The phone rings while I'm scooping ice cream into the blender.

"I just saw the paper," Mom says. "You look so mean, Travis."

"What do you mean I look mean?" I say. "Am I in there or something?"

"Right on the front page of the Sports section," Mom says.

"You're kidding," I say.

"Am not," she says. "It has you and Nathan's picture. Y'all and that Pineview boy's."

Nathan is Nathan Bass, my best friend. Nobody except Mom, his parents, and a couple of teachers ever calls him by his real name though. The rest of the world refers to him either as Lunk or the Lunker.

"Me and Lunk made the paper?" I say. "Amazing. What Pineview boy?"

"The one you've been so worried about," she says. "Jericho Dooms."

"Very funny, Mom," I say.

"I thought you might like that," she says. "I'm looking at him here and he's a handsome young man."

"Handsome?" I say.

"Don't you think so?" she says. "I mean really."

"I wouldn't know, Mom," I say. "I don't usually go around thinking about guys as being handsome or not handsome. It's not exactly my field. I haven't seen the paper yet anyway."

I hear her light a cigarette and exhale her first pull. I can see the smile she's making.

"You on break?" I say.

"Sort of," Mom says. "I'm about to cart the breakfasts around and I thought I'd sneak a smoke while I've got a minute to call my own. Plus I wanted you to know about your picture."

"Thanks," I say. "Especially for the part about how handsome Grooms is."

"Oh, he's not as handsome as you are, honey," she says.

"Never mind, Mom," I say. "Thanks for the toast too."

"You're welcome," she says. "Did Glen tell you where he was going to be today? I was wondering if he'll be off in time for that pep rally. I'd like to sit with him if I could."

"Last time I talked to him he said they were getting ready to clear a drilling site down around Winnfield," I say. "He was supposed to be hauling a 'dozer this morning, I think."

Mom doesn't say anything for a moment and I know that she's probably thinking about my daddy because I mentioned drilling. Daddy was a driller.

"Oh," she says. "Before I forget it, guess who had a baby a little while ago."

"Somebody I know?" I say.

"Somebody you had the biggest crush in the world on one time."

"Mrs. Hughes?" I say.

"Yep," Mom says. "Mrs. Hughes is a new mama this morning. It's a little boy. Jeff Junior. He's not so little actually. He weighed ten pounds and an ounce. The first thing Jeff said when he saw him was that he guessed he was a keeper."

Jeff Hughes runs a welding shop out on the highway. I spent the entire eighth grade wishing I was him because Mrs. Hughes was the best-looking, best-built teacher I ever had. I'd get light in the head watching her write biology facts on the board.

"Another Roughneck," I say.

"I would imagine so," Mom says. "Bless his heart. He has his little ball in there with him right now. Listen, I better get myself in gear before all these sick people start hollering about their food and drugs being late. Congratulations on the picture, Travis. I love you, hon. Good luck in the ball game if I don't get to talk to you again before it."

"OK, Mom," I say.

25

She hangs up. I never understood how she could do that but she always does. She never says good-bye.

I set the receiver down and the phone immediately rings again.

"Grand Central," I say.

"I hope you're ready, Cody," the caller says.

"Who is this?" I say.

I expect him to hang up as usual but he doesn't.

"Never mind that," he says.

"Don't you have the guts to at least tell me who you are?" I say.

"I got more guts than you'll ever have, boy," he says. "Who I am don't matter. All that matters is you lost that game for us last month and it cost me some money."

"You're nuts," I say.

"Just don't let it happen tonight, Cody," he says. "Do and you'll pay."

Then he hangs up, the cowardly bastard. I wish I knew who he was but I probably never will. Guys like him don't tell you their names or show you their faces. They're all talk, which is nothing. It's less than nothing, like their lives. I wonder if he's serious though. So far I haven't told anybody except Nita Tyler about these calls, but Nita doesn't count because she's my girl-friend and I tell her practically everything. I'm beginning to think that maybe I ought to let Glen know too. People are maniacs. First they call you on the phone, then they put a gun to your head. I don't think this character is that kind of dangerous but you never can tell. One thing I'm not going to do anymore today is answer the telephone. Anybody who has something to say to me will have to do it live and in person.

My stomach all of a sudden feels like I've swallowed a bird. It's in there fluttering around. This has been happening to me off and on all week. It got so bad at school on Wednesday morning that I caught Lyndon Garnett in the hall while we were changing classes for second period. Lyndon's our trainer and he carries a vial of butterfly tablets with him at all times.

"I need some pills for my nerves," I said.

Lyndon razzed me about it. He told me that Grooms was big and that Grooms was bad. He knocked his knees together and pretended to eat his fingernails like an ear of corn.

"Just shut up and come on, Lyndon," I said. "I'm not joking."

I felt bad about it later but I wasn't thinking about Grooms right then and I wasn't in the mood for any horsing around. What I was thinking about was the letter that had arrived in the mail the day before. It was from Dexter Tinsley, an assistant coach at Northwestern State down in Natchitoches, and it was a total shock. He told me that he was coming to Oil Camp on Saturday, mainly to look at a Pineview guy but also to look at me because he'd noticed my effort against Grooms while he was watching a tape of the November 20 game.

"Understand that I don't mean to get your hopes up, Travis," he wrote. "Quite frankly, you're too small for a college lineman. Nevertheless, we're always interested in young men with the kind of pride and desire you apparently possess. Because of this, there is a slight chance that we might be able to find a place for you in our program.''

I haven't even told Nita about that letter yet. It still seems unreal to me. Before I got it I'd pretty much accepted the fact that going to college right away was not a realistic possibility. My plan was to take a full-time job for a couple of years after graduation, then start night classes somewhere. But Coach Tinsley's letter has caused me to reconsider everything. My high school career hasn't exactly been a day at the lake, especially lately, and I've been looking forward to tonight because it's my last game almost as much as I've been looking forward to facing Grooms again. Now this news arrives and I'm looking at the possibility of padding up for four, maybe five more years. It seems incredibly ironic to me that, just when I've about decided that I've had enough of it, football could be what bails me out of having to postpone my main goal, which is to get a college degree. Nobody in my family ever has. The closest anyone has come is Mom with her registered nurse's diploma.

I could use a handful of Lyndon's pink disks right now. Breakfast is totally out of the question. I dump the ice cream into the sink and rinse the blender. The toast will keep. Mom can use it for dressing or something later. After I square away the kitchen I walk out into the cold to pick up our paper. Instead of bending I squat. I don't want to agitate my favorite ache. Back inside I pull out section C, less interested in seeing myself and Lunk than in seeing Grooms, which is no problem because his picture dominates the top half of the page.

He's in full gear except for his hat and he's posed in the posture of a middle linebacker: feet spread, shoulders squared, rear low, elbows bent, fingers fanned. Jesus. He looks great. His form is perfect and his face is impassive, like he's refusing to waste any energy at all for the photographer. I wouldn't think the word *handsome* if Mom hadn't put it in my head but I guess I'll have to admit that, yeah, old Grooms is a pretty handsome dude. He looks kind of like Lando Calrissian from the *Star Wars* movies.

The slightly less refined mugs of Lunk and me are to the right of the shot of Grooms. It's just our heads, our necks, and part of our shoulders. The caption runs beside us instead of below:

> Jericho Grooms (far left) and the top-ranked Pineview Pelicans will be looking to complete their season with an unblemished 14–0 record when they travel to Oil Camp for tonight's Class AA state championship game. Like Grooms, Oil Camp's Nathan Bass (top) and Travis Cody (bottom) will go both ways as the 12–1 Roughnecks seek to avenge their only loss of the year.

I've never made the Shreveport paper except by name. This is the Lunker's second appearance. We look like we're trying out for the bulletin board at the post office, a pair of genuine teenage desperadoes. The truth is that we're only squinting into strong sunshine.

These pictures of us were taken during Bataan, our August two-a-days. Mine's dated. I'm looking quite a bit older now than I did four months ago. I'm feeling that way too.

It's odd to discover myself staring out from an edition of a newspaper that hit yards, driveways, porches, and coin racks all over the north half of the state while I was sleeping. I always thought it would be a rush to get singled out like this but it's not. It's actually more of an embarrassment considering the way Grooms crushed me when everything was on the table on November 20. Guys in Pineview will probably see me and go, "Who is this Cody joker? Oh yeah. He's the granny my man Jericho misused on the two-point attempt. Nice try, chump. See *you* this evening." To which I can only reply, "Bring it on, fellows. Bring it on."

Nick Van Noate, who was responsible for the bad press I received last week, wrote the long preview story. It's headlined "Rivalry Renewed for Title Tilt" and it's wrapped around the cluster of pictures. Part of my game-day ritual is to read the preview story during study hall, third period. I'm always interested in seeing what Van Noate says about us and the other team but I'm also interested in seeing how he says it. He's a good writer as long as he sticks to the facts. I'm two paragraphs into today's piece before I catch myself and wonder if I've blown my routine. No way I did that. I turn to page 3 to check Nick's Picks. He's got Pineview by a touchdown, 14–7. I don't agree with the outcome but the score seems right. I've been thinking that one TD will decide it. Maybe my telephone buddy will go with Nick and give the points so he can root against me outright.

I fold section C and slip it inside the other two, then I lay the whole paper on Mom's place mat. She's been cutting out all the write-ups about us this season and arranging them in a scrapbook for me. She says that I'm going to treasure them whenever I get old enough to realize that this is the time of my life. Thinking about that reminds me of something Pawpaw once told me.

"Time don't have no brakes, Travis," he said. "You got to just hang on and ride her out. Maybe you'll wind up where you want to be, maybe you won't. Time don't care either way because time ain't nothing but full speed ahead. Know what else?"

"What?" I said.

"I'll tell you what," Pawpaw said. "About all you do when it gets right down to the blade is move from one ending to the next."

"That's not much of a deal, is it?" I said.

Pawpaw took his pipe from his mouth and drew his lips into a slight smile. A long moment passed before he responded.

"No," he said. "It ain't. But it's the only deal we got and you always feel one of two ways when you come to the end of something, don't matter how little or big whatever it is was. Listen to me good now, son, because this here is gospel. You either satisfied you done the best you could or regretful you didn't. I'm talking perspective, of course. Go in believing and most likely you'll come out just fine. Go in doubting and it's a different tale. See what I'm driving at?"

"Sort of," I said.

"Well, you will soon enough," Pawpaw said. "She moves at a smart pace, Travis, time does. She's never slown down for nobody I ever heard of and she won't be slowing down for you."

I was twelve years old then and it was my habit to pay close, hang-on-every-line attention to anything Pawpaw had to say because I was beginning to understand what it meant to know him. He was the only grown man in my life. My daddy, his son, had been dead for five years. I had Glen, who's four years older than I am, and Mom, who's Mom, but when Daddy got killed his absence left a space in me, a hole that nobody could fill. Pawpaw came close. He was like my father and my grandfather both, and I admired and looked up to him because he always seemed to know what he was talking about even when I didn't quite follow him. He had seen and done some things. He had been around.

What he said that day didn't make much sense to me at first. He seemed to be talking more to himself than to me anyway, but he put the concept into my head and it was there to stay. Now I do see what he meant. Life really is a series of events that run a course of a certain length then end. Nothing is forever except time and the idea that we are caught in it and have no control over its constant forward movement is something that has bothered me ever since I became aware of it. One of my fantasies is to be able to stop time altogether, to freeze it so that from then on I'd be released from it and wouldn't ever have to worry about it running out.

I wonder if this really is the time of my life. Four weeks ago I would have said no way, but now that it's almost over I'm not exactly doing back flips in celebration. Tomorrow all this will be history, archives, memory. The game will be won and lost. Coach Tinsley will have seen me do whatever it is I'm going to do. Then what? I'm determined to go to college someday and sooner or later I will. Other than that I don't know for sure. The only thing I know is that I hope my future doesn't turn me into the kind of guy who lives in the past. I like to think that I'll never even look at the scrapbook, that if anything I'll just be glad Mom bothered to make it for me.

I have one more thing to do before I leave the house. The tape is already cued. I feed it into the VCR and press the Play button. The tape whirs. I turn down the sound on the TV so I won't hear whoever was standing beside Mr. Arlen go, "Damnit, Cody. God *damnit,* Cody." Mr. Arlen, Oil Camp High's ag teacher, videos our games and I had him make me this copy of Pineview. I have no idea who was up on top of the press box with him that night. It could have been anybody.

I watch the play and run it back. I watch it again. One last time. I know every aspect of it. I saw something new each of the first few hundred times I reviewed it but now I have it down cold. I've tortured myself with it so often that it's locked in my brain forever.

Ejecting the tape I remind myself to read Van Noate's preview story sometime between ten and eleven, when I'd be in third period. I haven't looked at it yet, right? Nah. It never crossed my mind. My English teacher, Mr. Parke, would say that it doesn't matter either way because my destiny is already knitted. According to him superstition is a waste of time because rituals don't sway the Fates one way or the other. According to me they're a necessity because they make me feel better. The Fates aren't the only ones who are set in their ways.

4

This is my fourth Saturday in a row to be taking a seven o'clock spin to the stadium. None of the other three looked quite like this though. It's beautiful out here right now, chill with a clean early sky. The rays of the sun are just beginning to show behind the pines to the east and the soft light gives the landscape the appearance of a watercolor. It's a privilege to be out and about on a motorcycle on a morning like this. A car would be easier on my back and warmer, but I don't have a car and that wouldn't be quite the same anyway. Even though I'm freezing I like being in direct contact with such a fine morning.

At the stadium I'll do a whirlpool and then Grease, our manager, will wrap some heat on my back. He'll already be there when I arrive. You have to get up a lot earlier than I'm willing to if you want to beat the Greaser. He was even there last week. We pulled in from Cameron at three A.M. and Grease probably didn't get away for another hour. He was back before seven. He was in there doing the foul laundry we took from our travel bags and piled in front of our lockers before we went home. There were socks and jocks and half-shirts, towels and pads and thirty-two filthy black-on-gold road costumes.

It had rained in Cameron most of the week before our game and the field down there was torn up to start with. Most high school surfaces are a mess by playoff time but South Cameron's looked like it had been bombed. It was a scout team dream. Because of the rain all you had to do to look like a starter was go through pregame, which everybody who knew that he wouldn't play did with a purpose. The understudies were psyched. They wanted to wear some of that south Louisiana mud so they came after us like wildmen. The only reason I didn't get the redass about it like Lunk did was that I knew exactly how they felt. Being a three-year starter who has never been injured, Lunk has no idea what it's like to walk off the field wearing a clean uniform. I do. I've been there. I know just what it feels like and there's nothing worse. Failing to mark your game clothes reduces you. It's a sign that you weren't involved in the action. Nobody had that problem at Cameron though, because the whole team was caked before kickoff.

The Greaser does our wash immediately after every practice and the morning after every game. He's stronger than dirt. Grass stains don't stand a chance against him. Neither do blood and sweat. I'd say that he ought to do a detergent commercial but I know it wouldn't be convincing because he's a born mechanic and looks like one, which is why we've been calling him Grease for as long as I can remember. He's also the most loyal bud you could ever hope to have. Dial him at any hour and he'll answer the first ring. Tell him what you need and if he can't do something about it over the phone, he'll be on his way before you can thank him, no questions asked. He's a Good Samaritan in real life. Crews has said many times that Grease is the glue that holds us together and nobody disagrees. The Greaser is a friend indeed and a hero unsung, even if he does look like he combs his hair with Quaker State.

Downshifting I lean the bike slightly and make the turn onto the expanse of macadam between Roughneck Field and City Park. The seventh fairway of the golf course is visible in the distance, stretching brown and sandy through two rows of towering loblollies. The theater, as Stills once called it, is on my left. It's in excellent shape. We haven't used it in two weeks except for our Thursday walk-throughs and the one we did yesterday, and Mr. Arlen has had his Future Farmers working the turf every day for six straight periods. They've got it filled and groomed. Crews will chalk the yard lines later today. The rumor was that if we made the finals they were going to spray the dying grass of the playing field green before lining it. Some people actually believed that. Typical.

I reach down and kill my engine, coast up beside Grease's restored Corvair, and drop my kickstand. The rear window of the Corvair has TAKE STATE soaped on it. Seeing those words causes my gut to flutter again. I draw a deep breath and let it out as slowly as I can. The plume of it drifts away like a ghost. My face, hands, and toes are numb from the ride over. My lips have changed from flesh to ice. They'd probably shatter if I smiled. I hang my U.S. flag crash helmet on a mirror and try to make my way around to the gate without favoring my back. No dice. I have to stoop like an old man.

The dressing room is nice and warm. Grease must be down at the other end because he has the radio cranked. The box is tuned to the local station, KOYL, which will broadcast the replays of all our playoff games starting at eight. Meanwhile some country queen is detailing her miseries. Things haven't turned out the way she planned and I don't want to hear about it. Grease likes that tonk music. I don't mind it if I'm in a certain mood but right now I'm not in that mood. I'm in one that requests something historic from the other side of town. I load some Al Green into the machine and flip the lever to Tape. This is from the Stills collection, needless to say. Stills is our resident music expert as well as our quarterback and he says that nothing worth lending an undivided ear to has been recorded since the late seventies, disco being the beginning of the end. You can't argue with him either. I've heard some people try but Stills won't budge. He's dead set on his oldies thesis and he has a huge collection of albums, cassettes, and CDs to support it. Don't even mention rap to him. We had an oxymoron contest in Mr. Parke's class the other day and Stills submitted *rap music*. My All-Time Top 10 list grows every time I go to his house. The name is sort of a joke because I couldn't keep the list down to just ten if I had to. I hear something and if I like it it's on. Stills came up with the Al Green right after school started and as usual there was no disputing his taste. We've been playing it low after lights-out all season. It works loud too. Those horns break out of there so sweet. Stills says that Al Green is preaching in Memphis these days. I can see it. There's something holy about the way the man sings.

The smell in this room is a potent mixture of Pine Sol, Atomic Balm, and sweat, with a trace of dirty socks and mildew around the edges. It's not entirely pleasant but I love that smell. It helps me get in touch with what I'm here for. During the spring before our sophomore year the Touchdown Club raised money to have the floor carpeted and for a while all you could smell in here was that rug and the paste that kept it down. It wasn't right. A dressing room shouldn't smell of new carpet. A dressing room shouldn't smell of anything new. What a dressing room should smell of is something old and tough that reminds you of the fact that others have been in it before you and that they've paid the same price to play the game that you're paying. What a dressing room should smell of is tradition. You breathe it in and get inspired because you're connected. You're part of the past and the future at the same time. Tradition. That's what I smell in every corner of this room.

My locker is in a group of four that stand against the far wall. It's the one on the end near the door that leads to the concession area. We call them lockers but actually they're open cabinets made of sanded and sealed walnut. Each of them has a shelf for shoulder pads and pegs for jerseys and pants. Headgear goes on top. Everybody's last name and number are felt-marked on a strip of adhesive tape attached to the edge of his shoulder pad shelf. Whenever I'm in here by myself I'm always surprised by how incredibly neat our lockers are. The hats face forward and the shoes, practice and game, are lined up ready to march. It looks like thirty-two moms have come around and picked up after their boys. True credit belongs to Grease. He's got pride to spare.

The pegs are bare now. Grease will hang our game things on them later this morning. We'll wear our jerseys to the pep rally and our pants, leggings, jocks, and socks will be waiting for us when we come over after the pregame meal. Grease has spoiled us. I wouldn't do his job for good money. He does it for nothing.

I concentrate on Al Green as I undress. He's putting a move on the female population of the English-speaking world with "Let's Stay Together." He's setting them up with an irresistible tempo and finishing them off with gentle horns and promises. It's an All-Timer, high on my list.

I'm down to my socks and shorts when Grease slips in behind a basket of whites fresh from the dryer.

"You seen the paper yet?" he says.

It's the same question he opened with last Saturday. I give him the same response.

"Morning, Grease," I say. "Jock, please."

Grease sets his basket down and tosses me a warm supporter. I take my time putting it on and arranging myself because there's nothing the Greaser hates to see more than somebody moving slow. He's always in a big hurry to get to his next project, which in this case is going to be to give me some grief about getting my picture on page 1C this morning. Last week he brought the paper up because of the way Nick Van Noate described the safety South Cameron scored as a result of the slapstick routine Lunk and I performed on that late punt. I know the paragraph by heart:

> The Tarpons' only points came with just over five minutes remaining in the contest when Oil Camp's Travis Cody missed the ball on a punt from his own end zone. The play, a comedy of errors as Cody retrieved the ball and scrambled back and forth in search of an opening that wasn't there, ended abruptly when South Cameron's Randall Broussard nailed the rattled kicker for a safety.

There was more fiction than journalism in that account. First, I didn't miss the ball. Second, I wasn't rattled. What actually happened was that Lunk, the middle of our three up-backs on punts, just plain forgot what he was doing and stepped back to pass-block after the snap. He was supposed to hold his ground for a three-count then release. The ball, which I kicked just fine, hit him square in the glutes after traveling maybe six inches off my foot, *thadap*. I had my head down but I immediately knew what had happened and turned to find the ball. When I picked it up I started right, thinking that I could still get it away. The end had me fenced though, so I went left. Seeing that I was dead over there too, I decided to quit messing around and just down it. That's when the South Cameron guy stuck me.

Crews gnawed on me a little for not covering the ball in the first place, but the game was pretty much in the book by then so I didn't get full wrath until the

Monday movies. Crews never rants and raves at us during a game. He leaves that to Wroten, his assistant. Wroten is one of those hot-wired guys who takes everything anybody does wrong personally. His favorite sound is that of his own voice saying something negative. I thought he was going to strangle Lunk on the sideline before he got through. I waited my turn but he let me slide. About all he said to me was that I had less brains than his two-year-old daughter.

"That was six rolling around back there, Cody," he said.

Wroten's too strung. He got mad at Lunk all over again on Monday and made him run punishment stadiums before *and* after practice. I skipped the first session but I joined in on the second. Wroten couldn't believe it. He said that I didn't have the sense God gave a pinecone. I don't guess he's ever had a friend. If he had he might have understood what I was doing.

The point is that I'm not sure what event Van Noate thought he was watching. Maybe he wasn't watching at all. Maybe he looked away for a second, didn't see what happened, and took a wild guess. All I know is that everybody I ran into last weekend had something to say about the fantasy paragraph. They got a lot of mileage out of it. Some, like my boss, Mr. Shackleford, are still on me about it.

"Can't you do that any slower?" Grease says.

"I'm in pain, G," I say. "Remember? That's how come I'm here."

"I'm in pain too," Grease says. "What's that outdated mess doing on my jukebox?"

"It's educational," I say. "Timeless too. Listen and learn some history, son. I saw the paper."

Grease grins so hugely that I check to see if any of his places ooze. His skin is a disaster. Luck of the draw. He wears some serious flare-ups.

"First your name then your picture," he says. "Next they'll be doing a feature. You paying somebody over there or what?"

"Maybe I have a guardian angel or something," I say.

Grease presents a palm. I oblige.

"They must've felt bad after I called them," he says.

"Come again?" I say.

"I'm your guardian angel," Grease says. "I called up the paper on the phone and told them they ought to send somebody who can see to cover our games. I don't know if it was Van Noate or who that I was talking to, but I said you didn't miss that ball and that it wasn't fair for them to say you did. I wasn't going to tell you, but what the hell."

Grease. I almost hug him. He's such a total bud.

"Catch," he says.

I one-hand the towel he throws, twirl it a few times, and snap it at his crotch. He steps aside. All the little Greasers are saved.

"Thanks, man," I say.

"I didn't have nothing to do with the picture," Grease says. "That was their idea."

"That's not what I'm thanking you for, bonehead," I say.

"A check's fine then," Grease says. "But I do take Visa and MasterCard. Water's ready when you are."

He ejects Al Green and turns the radio back on as he leaves. An ad for the replay of the playoff games is running.

"Go 'Necks," Grease says.

"Drill 'em," I say.

In the whirlpool room I read the gauge and glance at the clock on the brick partition that separates the trio of johns and the trough from this area. I ease my feet into the tub. The jets are wide open. Still water at this temperature is uncomfortable at first. In motion it takes your breath away and I have to get all the way down in it. I watch the second hand sweep around the face of the clock. Sweat breaks out on my forehead. I take the plunge.

Haya.

Grease will fetch me in fifteen minutes. He'll cover a square cut from a Pampers with gooey balm and wrap it against my lower back with an Ace bandage. Lyndon taught him a few rudimentary training tricks for extra-early Saturday morning patients. Dr. L rarely makes the stadium before eight.

Reclining so that the gush of incoming water meets me where I'm troubled, I close my eyes and chase all visions of failure and shadows of doubt out of my mind with a reverie about Nita Tyler, who is the best answer I know of to one part of the old saying that nothing is ever as good or as bad as it seems. Nita told me last summer that she wouldn't mind being my valentine for life. The way she said it and the way she looked when she said it, with her head tilted back and the ends of her damp hair tangled up in my fingers as we leaned against a pine in first dark after a day at the lake—well, let's just say that these things were every bit as good as they seemed.

Thinking about that day suddenly reminds me of one of the few dreams I've had lately that Grooms didn't either star or make a cameo appearance in. It featured a blue sky, a green lake, and my dark-eyed girlfriend looking too fine for language in an all-white Body Glove swimsuit. She was running toward me, but I woke up before she got there and the whole scene immediately vanished. I completely forgot about it until just now, which is strange. The timing is excellent though, and as the vision reconstructs itself I feel the knotted muscles in my back begin to relax. I can't hear what's on the radio from here so I let my mind take its pick. It goes for the obvious, a sultry number from Bob Seger and the Silver Bullet Band called "Come to Papa."

I grin. If Nita were here reading my thoughts she'd shake her head and roll her eyes.

"Guys," she'd say. "Y'all are so pathetic."

Nita and I began moving out of the just-friends stage last summer. We're not all the way out of it yet but I've got enough sense not to push her past where she wants to go. Sometimes it isn't easy though. Sometimes being patient with her is the most frustrating thing I've ever had to do. But she's patient with me too so we're fairly even in the give-and-take department. We make a pretty good pair.

5

I'm wrapped up snug and tight and I'm smelling from here to the Gulf of Mexico of Atomic Balm. My back is burning at skin level but the muscles are at ease. I feel young and strong again. I'm not stooping. Grease walks me to the door.

"Tell me a joke," I say.

Grease is always good for a joke. He collects them, mostly groaners.

"OK," he says. "Know why nobody in Pineview makes chocolate chip cookies?"

"Not really," I say.

"Because they think it's too much trouble to peel the M&M's," he says.

"That's pretty pitiful, Grease," I say.

"It's pretty early, Cody," Grease says.

"Lame excuse," I say. "You still owe me one."

"I'll see what I can do," he says.

I touch the SACRIFICE sign as I open the door, aware that it's not quite the purely automatic gesture it was a month ago.

"Later on," I say. "Don't work too hard."

"I'll try not to," Grease says.

I close the door behind me and move to the gate. I walk through it but then I hear something that makes me stop and turn around. I can see part of the field, the south goalpost, the scoreboard, and a section of the east-side bleachers. A sheen of frost decorates the playing surface but the sun, which is riding a hard blue sky this morning, will erase that directly.

I stand still and listen.

In a clearing between the road that flares to become the parking lot and the fence that borders the field beyond the north end zone are an old Lufkin pumping unit and a small storage tank. Both of them are painted the same shade of gold as our road uniforms, new gold, and on the storage tank in black block letters are the words ROUGHNECK PRIDE. I can't see them from where I'm standing but I can hear the engine that drives the pumping unit. The sound is like a part of me because I've been hearing it all my life. I don't even notice it most of the time, the way I don't notice my heart. It's just there, doing what it does. But the grinding whine of that engine figures into my earliest memories and whenever I become aware of it, I think of my daddy because he used to drive me by there in his truck when I was little. I remember sitting on his lap behind the big steering wheel. We'd park and I'd watch the strange machine go up and down while he sipped Dixie beer from a can and thought his thoughts. The pumping unit looked like a living thing to me. It seemed to be trying to free itself and I worried about it. Mom says that I called it the o-wee-wee because I couldn't say "oil well." Later, in one of my summertimes, I discovered that I could hear the engine faintly crying in the nighttime distance through my open window. The o-wee-wee never got away.

Daddy. I don't have enough memories of him and most of the ones I do have are vague. They're like scenes from a movie I saw a long time ago. I once asked Mom if she thought I'd be much different if he'd been around longer.

"No," she said. "You're turning out just like him anyway."

I loved that answer because I knew it was a compliment. It made me proud.

My folks were high school sweethearts. They married each other the summer after they graduated. Daddy went straight to work in the oil field and Mom checked groceries at the Piggly Wiggly. Daddy started out as a roughneck on a Marathon crew Pawpaw put together and he'd worked himself up to derrick hand by the time Glen was born. He was a driller when I came along. He had his own crew and the money he made as a boss was what eventually helped Mom decide to quit her job at the store and start commuting to LSU-Shreveport three days a week to study nursing. They weren't ever going to be anywhere near rich but they were beginning to get ahead. They were making it. They were steadily building a comfortable life for themselves in their hometown.

The accident that changed everything happened on a day when my daddy was off work. A friend of his named Dale Perkins called him that afternoon and said he had a load of crossties he needed to deliver to a spot on the railroad up by the state line. He was planning to unload the ties and then go shoot a few racks of pool, which he and Daddy liked to do together. It was July. Glen was at Scout camp and Mom was at work. Daddy asked me if I minded him leaving for a while. I didn't because I was on my way to Lunk's anyway. The last thing Daddy ever said to me was, "Tell your mother I'll be home in time for supper." I'll never forget that. I was only seven years old but those words will be with me forever.

Tell your mother I'll be home in time for supper.

Lunk and I were up in his tree house sorting football cards when we heard the sirens.

"Let's follow them," Lunk said.

"Is that the fire one or what?" I said.

"Sounds more like the ambulance to me," Lunk said. "Whatever it is, it's got the police with it too."

"Maybe it's a wreck," I said.

We rode our bicycles in the direction of the sirens, but they were on the highway headed out of town so we turned back and pedaled over to the swimming pool. We were eating snow cones and watching some high school guys play Ping-Pong when Mr. Belcher, who managed the pool, walked out and told me that I needed to go with him.

"Why?" I said. "Where to?"

"Just come go with me, son," Mr. Belcher said.

"Can I too?" Lunk said.

"You better stay," Mr. Belcher said.

"I'll call you," I said.

"Hope everything's OK," Lunk said.

I handed him what was left of my snow cone and

followed Mr. Belcher. He drove his car like he was in a race. At first I didn't say anything and neither did he. We were going way over the speed limit and I was scared but not of that. I was thinking of Pawpaw. Something awful must have happened to him. I stood not talking for as long as I could, then I had to know what was going on.

"There's been an accident, Travis," Mr. Belcher said. "That's all I can say."

"Who?" I said.

Mr. Belcher clenched his teeth and shook his head.

"Tell me who," I said. "Please, Mr. Belcher."

He wouldn't do it though.

"I'm sorry, Travis," he said. "It's just not my place. I don't want to say anything that might not be right."

My heart was hammering when we turned in at the hospital. I don't even remember getting out of the car.

Mom was sitting on a couch in the freezing-cold waiting area outside the emergency room. She had on her nurse's uniform with the little cap. Pawpaw was standing beside her. One of his hands was on her shoulder. Mom looked small and dazed and Pawpaw looked like he'd lived twenty years since I saw him that morning.

"Oh, Travis," Mom said.

She put her arms out. I went to her. She hugged me tight and I could feel her shaking. I heard Mr. Belcher ask Pawpaw what the chances were.

Pawpaw cleared his throat.

"Not worth a damn," he said.

Mom took a deep, ragged breath. Without letting go she pushed me away from her. She squeezed my upper arms until I thought her fingernails were going to cut through my skin. Her eyes were red and her face was wet.

"Daddy's been hurt real bad, honey," she said.

She tried to say something else but she couldn't do it. All she could do was pull me to herself again and hold me. She kept patting me on the back. I felt numb.

Daddy died that night. Mr. Perkins had been killed instantly. Nobody knew exactly what happened but Pawpaw always said that the crossties must have either been overbalanced to start with or shifted in transit. They were held down by a pair of heavy chains and it was likely that when Mr. Perkins released the second binder, the load came off the trailer like it was on a spring. Mr. Perkins was directly under it and Daddy was two or three paces behind him. Neither one of them had time to react.

Still listening to the whine of the pumping unit engine, I look over at the scoreboard. Everything on it is digital except the clock, which is notorious and probably one of the last of its kind in use these days. It's a big white disk with a black 0 at the top. To the right of the 0 is a 12 and to the left of the 0 is a 1. Between them, going right and around are 11, 10, 9, 8, 7, 6, 5, 4, 3, and 2. These are the minutes, kept by a short black hand. On the edge of the circle are three-inch slashes, also black, numbered from 59 back to 1. These are the seconds, kept by a long red hand. It's a bear of a clock to decipher if you're not used to it. Opposing coaches have been complaining about it for the past few years but I doubt that it will ever be replaced. It's part of the mystique of Roughneck Field, where Oil Camp has never lost more than two home games during a season since Crews became head coach in the late sixties. Daddy and Glen knew that clock as well as I do. They were in many a contest that it timed.

I've watched the films of all of Daddy's games and the tapes of Glen's, which I saw in person. Both of them were bigger than I am but I may be a little bit quicker. That would be my only advantage. Daddy played tackle both ways, like Glen, who wore his number. Being a center I'm supposed to have one in the fifties but Crews gave me 77 because he knew the link. I didn't even have to ask him.

"Wear it well, Cody," he said. "Your relatives did."

"I know it," I said. "I'll try."

Daddy was a three-year starter. Glen was a sub as a sophomore but he got his three letters. They both made All-District as seniors. I missed my junior letter because of my elbow so I'll only finish with two, sophomore and senior. I was thinking All-District before this season started but thanks to Grooms that won't happen unless I make it for punting, which is a lot different from making it at center or noseguard. Grooms will get the honors at my real positions and he deserves to. He'll also be All-State at one or both of them and he has a good shot at Class AA Player of the Year on defense. What can I say? He's the best, which is why he's been courted by heavyweight programs since before he moved to Louisiana. I'm just a slightly above average country ballplayer with an outside chance at getting an offer from a small school that I'm not even sure I want. I'm no Grooms, nowhere near it. I haven't embarrassed my number though. Take away one play from the disaster of four weeks ago and I've worn it pretty well.

I glance at the clock again. Right now the red hand is set on 0, the black one on 12. They're waiting to count down my last forty-eight minutes of high school ball. Take State. Daddy helped do it as a sophomore and as a junior and his senior team came within six points of making it three straight. Glen helped do it as a junior. After that black hand over there has backed from the 12 to the 0 four more times I'll either be able to say that I helped do it as a senior or not. Time will tell. It always does and it never lies. The clock rolls. Zero eventually comes. It's inevitable. There's no way to stop it, though occasionally I wish I could.

I got into a big discussion about this with Mr. Parke during English yesterday. We'd been looking at a sonnet by William Shakespeare that had to do with the passage of time and getting old.

"Time is undefeated," Mr. Parke said. "It passes and it carries us along with it. All of us are moving toward whatever it is that fate has in store for us. Some of us will live through four full seasons. Like the narrator of this poem we'll have our spring, our summer, our fall, and our winter. Others won't be as fortunate, assuming that living to old age is a fortunate thing."

I was sitting there thinking about Pawpaw and Daddy. One died old and the other died young. Neither of them was fortunate in the end though. Pawpaw was bad sick during his last six months and Daddy just got cut down before he should have. I recalled what Pawpaw had said that day about time not having any brakes and before I could stop myself I raised my hand. Mr. Parke gave me the floor and I said that I thought it would be a great thing to be able to live outside of time.

"They say it's a curse but to me that's just like saying it's a curse to come into a bunch of money," I said. "I believe I could handle either one. At least I wouldn't mind getting a chance to find out."

Mr. Parke's eyes widened the way they will whenever somebody brings up something he wants to pursue.

"OK," he said. "Economics aside, let us say that you have been granted this other ability, Travis. Let us say that you have the power to stop time. Now. Doesn't this imply that you can only do it once?"

Mr. Parke reads real Greek and studies the ancient philosophers. His hero is Socrates and he likes to make everything into a question. He leads you into traps if you're not careful but he always helps you look at stuff in a way you never have before. He's about five five and weighs maybe 130 but he seems a lot bigger. Sometimes he seems like a giant to me because he's so wise.

"I suppose it does," I said.

"Would you be willing to do it?" he said.

It was as if all of a sudden nobody else was in the room. That's one of Mr. Parke's best attributes as a teacher and as a person. Once you have his attention you have it completely.

"It depends," I said.

"On what?" he said.

"On the situation," I said.

"Isn't the situation your life?" he said.

"I don't know what you mean," I said.

"What I mean is simply that if you can do it, you can do it only once and that once would end your life at that point. You exist in time and if time stopped you would cease to exist along with it. Correct or incorrect?"

"Correct," I said. "I guess."

"Don't guess," Mr. Parke said. "Am I correct or incorrect?"

"You're correct," I said.

"Good. Are you willing then to abbreviate your life in order to exercise this special power of yours?"

"I wouldn't go that far."

"But don't you have to?"

I looked around the room.

"Feel free to bail me out anytime, y'all," I said.

"I think you're on your own here, Codysan," Stills said.

"Yeah," Lunk said. "Just be sure to wake me up when this is over. I'm coming down with a bad case of boredom. Sorry, Mr. P. I mean *indifference.*"

Mr. Parke waited for everybody to quit laughing. He won't let us use any form of the word *boring* in his classroom. He says that only brain-dead people allow themselves to become bored.

"Nice recovery, Nathan," he said. "So. What is the one thing that we know about time, Travis?"

"That it's always in motion," I said.

"Besides that," Mr. Parke said.

"That it's relative," I said.

"Exactly," he said. "And what does that mean?" He was smiling. I shrugged.

"That it only seems to fly or go slow but it never really does?" I said.

Mr. Parke nodded his head vigorously, which is what he always does when he has you where he wants you. I shifted in my seat.

"Time moves at a constant rate," Mr. Parke said. "The circumstances of the individual only seem to speed it up or slow it down as the case may be. Now. How would you characterize your circumstances, Travis? Generally speaking."

"My circumstances seem to speed it up," I said. "Generally speaking. It moved slower for me than it ever has when I was hurt last year but now it's going pretty fast."

"You're lucky then," Mr. Parke said.

"How come?" I said.

"Pardon the cliché but one way of putting it would be to say that time is flying for you because you're having fun," he said. "That's why you'd like to slow it down. You want to savor what's happening."

"Which is a paradox," I said. "Right?"

"Explain," Mr. Parke said.

"It goes slow when you want it to go fast and it goes fast when you want it to go slow," I said.

The bell rang.

"Excellent," Mr. Parke said. "Class dismissed. Come here a second before you leave, Travis."

I followed him to his desk. He sat down and leaned back in his chair.

"Interesting dialogue," he said.

"Confusing," I said.

"Don't give me that," he said. "You had some very impressive responses. I do have one more question about the relativity of time for you though."

"Shoot," I said.

"If it flies when you're having fun and creeps when you're not, what I want to know is: How's it going to move for Jericho Grooms tomorrow night? Think you can make it creep for him?"

"Are you serious?" I said.

"Completely," he said.

"I'm going to try," I said.

"Can you?" he said. "Yes or no."

"Yes," I said.

I tried to make it sound like I meant it because I knew that's what he wanted. As much as anything else, Mr. Parke is a motivator. He'd make a good coach.

"Let the other guy be the one who worries about that clock, Travis. Have some fun out there. Speed it up for yourself and slow it down for him. You can enjoy the memory of it and wish it hadn't all happened so fast later."

"Later's not the point," I said. "Later's too late. I wasn't even talking about that anyway."

"I know. At least you didn't think you were. But it's no secret that this confrontation is a huge moment for you. You've anticipated it and now it's at hand. What you were talking about, whether you realize it or not, is one of the central dilemmas of being human."

"Which is what?" I said.

"Which is that you're trapped in time and can't escape," he said. "Thus your fantasy."

"I'd do it if everything was exactly right," I said.

"Tough call," he said. "Wouldn't you be afraid of missing out on something even better?"

"It's just a fantasy," I said.

"Nothing wrong with that," Mr. Parke said. "Nothing at all."

I check the scoreboard clock again and imagine myself pancaking Grooms on our first play. Right now I can't think of anything in the world that could be much better than that.

6

My cycle is a little Honda 250 Nighthawk. It's candy apple red, waxed to where flies have a hard time landing on it, and paid for in full. I laid cash money on the counter for it down in Minden last May. The bike had just over four thousand miles on the odometer when I got it and I've added another fourteen hundred or so, but it looks better now than it did the day I picked it up. It looks like it never left the showroom in the first place because washing it is one of my favorite pastimes. I keep it spic and I keep it span. Grease, who couldn't care less how a machine looks, tutors me in the art of keeping it humming.

One of these years I'm going to own a Harley-Davidson Sportster 883, which I regard as a high-water mark of Western civilization. Sportsters almost always catch hell from the magazine test riders but there's something about their design that gets to me beyond being able to explain it to anybody. It's a look that's clean, simple, and somehow feminine to me. I can't get enough of it. I don't have any problems with the way they handle either. I've ridden two and the word that comes closest to describing the sensation I got from both of them is *celestial*. I kept waiting for the telltale flaws, but if any were there I didn't notice. I was too busy ascending into heaven.

My calendar has three Sportsters. March, June, and September. March and June are customs, which to me is like too much makeup on a girl who's pure cane to start with. It's degrading. September is straight off the line though, and that's the one I tore off and tacked to my closet door. Primitive Lunk has naked women on his. I've got a stock Sportster.

I guide the Nighthawk onto the concrete apron of Shackleford's Texaco. Mr. Shackleford bustles out of the lube bay and follows me over to my parking place. He's a case. He's tall and gawky, seems to be made out of parts that don't match, and looks like he's coming apart when he walks. He probably has sixty-five years behind him. This morning he's wearing an old green sweater that's sprung, blue pants, and a Russian-style fur hat that has faded from black to gray. Without waving or nodding or acknowledging me in any way, he steps around to where I have to watch and starts doing a mime of a punter. He extends his arms, crouches, takes an imaginary snap, drops the imaginary ball, and swings his right leg. But instead of admiring an imaginary spiral as it sails into the sky, he bobs his head and follows the imaginary ball as it bounces off to one side.

I sit with my arms folded. It's not easy to keep from smiling but I'm trying to. Mr. Shack is comical to me no matter what he does. He reminds me of a bird that didn't evolve quite enough to overcome gravity.

All he lacks is feathers. He goes through his ridiculous antics again, then he slaps his thighs. He has cracked himself up and his smile is like a baby's because he doesn't have his dentures in.

"That's hilarious, Mr. Shack," I say. "You ought to be on *Star Search*."

Mr. Shack moves in and whacks me on the shoulder. His eyes are dancing behind the thick lenses of his glasses.

"Come inside and let me buy you a cup of coffee, Young Cody," he says. "It's cold as a week-old polar bear turd out here."

Mr. Shackleford has always called me Young Cody. I've been working for him for nearly four years. The summer I started I had applied for a job sacking at the Piggly Wiggly but it didn't happen. Mom knew everybody down there and Glen, who was a senior, was still stocking for them so things were looking pretty good. But I had just turned fourteen and in the end they decided that I wasn't old enough. I asked Mr. Frazier, the manager, about maybe sweeping out or something part-time but he said he was sorry, he just didn't have anything for a fourteen-year-old.

"No hard feelings, Travis," he said. "You're just a little green. Come see me in a year or two."

I told him I sure would, but I was thinking that I couldn't wait that long. I was moving into the first phase of my life where I needed more money than I was willing to ask Mom or Pawpaw for so I had to get a job. Finding one in Oil Camp was a problem I didn't have any idea how to solve once the Piggly Wiggly deal fell through.

Fate in the form of a low tire bailed me out. The rear one on my bicycle needed air so I rode over to the Texaco to put some in it. Mr. Shackleford was checking gallon figures when I coasted in. He'd bend over and squint then he'd straighten up, write something into a notebook, lick his pencil, and move to the next pump to repeat the procedure. I kept an eye on him while I filled my tire. I knew that "Big Daddy" Yelvingston was his only help and I didn't think it would hurt to ask him if he could use another hand.

"Whale of an idea," Mr. Shackleford said.

He looked at me for a moment, then he looked at his hands. He studied the backs of them and he studied the palms.

"Yep," he said. "I do believe I could use me another one, Young Cody. Two ain't never been enough."

I went ahead and laughed.

"Extra help," I said.

"Oh," Mr. Shackleford said.

He seemed disappointed.

"Now that's a toad of a considerably different wart, Young Cody," he said. "You had me going for a second there. I was thinking maybe you'd come up with a secret formula to help a man grow himself a new paw."

"Sorry," I said.

Winking at me he took a pouch of Levi Garrett from his back pocket. He dug a hunk of stringy tobacco out of it, then he narrowed his eyes and appraised me. He looked me over good as he planted the chew in his mouth. It made me jumpy, but I kept my eyes on his and stood as tall as I was able to.

"Come to think of it there, Young Cody, I believe I might just could," Mr. Shackleford said at last. "Matter of fact I been threatening to take myself out a notice about it in the Weekly Wiper, otherwise known as the local paper. Why come you to ask?"

"I'm looking for a job," I said.

"Merciful," Mr. Shackleford said. "How in the world old are you these days?"

"I just made fourteen," I said.

Mr. Shackleford spat.

"Let's us go see about something then," he said. "Come with me over here."

He headed toward the garage. I coiled up the air hose and hung it back on its hook. A burgundy Lincoln turned off the street and pulled in for gas, sounding the station bell twice. I looked around for Big Daddy but he wasn't there. I pushed my bicycle over to the garage and waited for Mr. Shackleford. He came out carrying a sledgehammer and a crowbar.

"You plan to get that customer now or after a while?" he said.

"Me?" I said.

"I don't see nobody else," Mr. Shackleford said. "Check that oil for him too."

He put his hand on a tractor tire that was leaned against the building and pulled it over. I didn't move. I watched the big tire spin and settle. Mr. Shackleford spat.

"Well, go on, son," he said. "You can't work here and stand around at the same time."

My heart was double-timing as I approached the Lincoln.

"Fill it," the customer said. "Premium."

He had on a gray suit and plenty of aftershave lotion. His thick silver hair wouldn't have budged in a tornado. He looked like a politician.

"Yessir," I said.

I removed the nozzle from the pump, which automatically rang it down, then I impersonated somebody who had half a clue about where the gas tank on a Lincoln Continental was located. The customer asked me if there was a rest room he could use.

"Probably so," I said.

I didn't take my eyes off the car.

"Is it locked?" the customer said.

"What?" I said.

I was standing there holding the nozzle with one hand and the hose with the other.

"The rest room," the customer said. "Assuming that you have one. Is it locked or is it open?"

"How should I know?" I said. "I don't even work here. God. I must be blind."

The gas flap was on the left rear fender. It was so obvious that it had evaded me. Opening it I decided to quit while I was ahead and not try to check his oil.

"Beg pardon?" the customer said.

"Just go see that man yonder, mister," I said. "He knows. He owns the place."

"He asked me if you was retarded," Mr. Shackleford said after the customer drove away. "I told him the jury was still deliberating."

"Well, I'm not," I said.

"Don't get your dobber up," Mr. Shackleford said. "Here."

He handed me the tools. I'd never used a sledge before.

"Tire's flat. You pull it off the rim and I'll slap a patch on it. Hole's already marked."

"I don't know how," I said.

"Time to learn then," Mr. Shackleford said.

It didn't take me but two hours. I spent thirty minutes walking around trying to decide on a strategy and ninety minutes executing it. The sledge felt strange. It was top-heavy and hard to handle. I tried to work without it but the tire was stuck to the rim and had to be whacked again and again before it moved. I needed to be violent and delicate at the same time. Mr. Shackleford checked my progress every so often.

"Having fun?" he said after about an hour and a half.

"What do you think?" I said.

"I think you're setting a record."

"I'm not surprised," I said.

When I finally got one side of the tire separated from the rim I worked the crowbar around and lifted it off. The other side was easier but my hands were bleeding and my T-shirt was soaked with sweat by the time I finished. I sat down to rest. I closed my eyes. After a few minutes I felt something nudging me. It was the toe of one of Mr. Shackleford's boots.

"Already sitting down on the job," he said. "Don't make a habit of it."

He was holding a bottle of Nehi Red and a green bill cap with the Texaco star sewn on its crown. He presented them to me.

"According to the law of the land you a year away from old enough to hire," he said. "But the way I figure it, anybody who can break a tractor tire down ought to be exempt from all that foolishness. I'll fret over the government regulations if you'll be on time and stay on your feet while you're here. Deal?"

"Deal," I said.

I rode home not knowing exactly when "on time" was because I was so excited about getting a job that I forgot to ask. I didn't sleep more than an hour that night for fear of being late, but I was the first one at the station the next morning by forty-five minutes.

"You could've just called," Mr. Shackleford said. "I'd have told you for a fair price."

What I mainly do at the station is watch the front. I pump gas, check under hoods, and clean windshields. I also do the occasional lube and oil change, fix the occasional flat, and take care of the insides of cars and trucks after Big Daddy washes them. "Big Daddy" Yelvingston has been at Shackleford's Texaco since Day One. He's an ace mechanic in addition to being our official washer of vehicles so he spends most of his time in the garage and the wash bay. The reason he wasn't at the station the day I did the tractor tire, which is his other job, is that he was fishing. Big Daddy keeps Wednesdays to himself and he uses them for fishing regardless of the weather.

I have one more responsibility and that is to keep the station rest rooms gleaming. We do have them and they stay unlocked. Sometimes I wish we didn't. Public rest rooms are a disgrace to the human race, especially the female half.

Mr. Shackleford told me I was an SSA at the end of my first full day.

"That's Service Station Attendant frontwards," he said. "And it's ASS backwards. You can be either one."

He didn't say it like a joke and I didn't take it like one because I didn't know yet that Mr. Shackleford has more corn at his disposal than the Jolly Green Giant. I should have known because of the bad line he'd thrown me about another hand the day before but I didn't. I thought I must have ticked him off somehow and made him think that hiring me was a mistake.

"I'll try not to be an ass, Mr. Shackleford," I said.

I was so serious that my eyes were watering. Mr. Shackleford howled. He laughed like it was the funniest thing he'd ever heard anybody say.

"I don't think you're capable of being an ass, Young Cody," he said. "I'm glad to have you down here."

Saturday is my only full day at the station during the school year. It used to mean sleeping late, cartoons, and vacant-lot ball games. Now it means dipsticks, gluey windshields, and public rest rooms. It also means a paycheck and that was the original point. We're closed on Sunday but I pick up some hours after practice Monday, Tuesday, and Wednesday evenings. Mr. Shack pays me a dollar and a half an hour more than he has to. Even when I was injured and couldn't do much he did that. This year he started slipping me a ten every Saturday after games if he was satisfied with how I played. I've never asked and he's never said. I either find the bill in the breast pocket of my coveralls or I don't. Sometimes I'm surprised by his assessment. I thought I played well enough against Mansfield, for instance, but evidently Mr. Shack didn't agree. On the other hand I wouldn't have given myself ten after my November 20 encounter with Grooms. But then I'm not Mr. Shackleford. I guess he decided to look at the game as a whole and not put as much weight on one play as I did. All he said about that was: "Crews should have passed on the conversion."

I just nodded.

I've talked to Mr. Shackleford about moving to full-time at the station after I graduate. He said he'd love to have me but added that I could get myself set up for college faster if I hired on in the oil field.

"It ain't altogether dry, Young Cody," he said. "You might want to ask around about something in the way of production and maintenance, which would cut your saving-up time at least in half relative to what you'd make here. Glen knows everybody you'd need to see and Lord knows they all knew your daddy and granddaddy so you're three steps ahead of the pack already."

When I was younger I wanted to work in the patch and assumed I would. Now I understand what that really means and I'd rather avoid it if possible. I may wind up out there anyway though, at least temporarily. But I haven't looked into it yet because it's such an iffy deal these days and because I keep hoping I won't have to. Maybe Coach Tinsley will bail me out. Maybe he'll come to our dressing room after the game tonight and offer me a scholarship to his school so I can get on with my life. I'm thinking of the oil field as my last resort—no offense, Pawpaw and Daddy. I just know how much I'd hate it.

Inside, the KOYL replay of our first-round playoff game with Oak Grove is starting on the radio beside the new two-pot Bunn-O-Matic that rules the counter behind Mr. Shack's chaotic desk. Paul Maddox is at the mike along with Gilbert Dees. They're discussing our loss to Pineview in the regular season finale and its possible ramifications. Drums thump in the background.

Maddox owns the Ben Franklin on Main Street. He's a pale, dumpy man who doesn't look like he could tell the difference between a hash mark and a goal line, which is not the case at all. He knows football as well as anybody around here and he's been calling Oil Camp games since before my daddy played. His signature remark is ''Holy Moses!'' You'll find a lot of headphones in the stands when the Roughnecks play because Maddox sees more of what's going on than most people. He's a good companion.

Dees isn't bad either, except that he has a funny voice. It's like Glen said one time: "Gil talks like he just left his tongue on a Popsicle." Dees runs the oil field service Glen works for. He started doing games with Maddox after the Okie Colbert fiasco. Okie used to be Maddox's color man. One night he got so exercised over a punt return at Arcadia that he completely forgot where he was. The runner broke a tackle at the twenty and cut to one of the sidelines. His blockers had set up a perfect wall and he moved behind it. Okie, who'd undoubtedly been into the Old Crow on the way down there, jumped up, knocked his chair over, and yelled, "Jesus Lee Christ! Somebody put that little piss-ant on his goddamn butt!" into a live microphone. I was in junior high when he did it and I remember people saying that we weren't going to have a radio station anymore because Okie Colbert cussed. The only thing that ended up happening was a lifetime ban from the booth for Okie.

You see him around town, walking usually but sometimes driving his truck. He paints houses for a living and he comes to every game, home or away. He's one of those guys who stays right with the ball at all times. There's a big gang of them and they move along the fence. I know some of them by name but mostly they're just faces. They're always into the game and they pass judgment on every play. You'll be in on a stop over by where they are and you'll hear about it one way or the other every time. They won't hesitate to let you know what they think.

"You a puss, Cody," they'll say after one down. "Go buy yourself a dress, wimp. This ain't ballet lessons. *Stick* somebody."

"Way to be, Cody," they'll say after another. "Hand him back his strap if he's got anything left to put in it."

I'd rather be shot dead right here and now than end up like that. Some of them are only a few years out of high school but already they're so lost that all they can do is get drunk, stand at the fence, and remember. You act like you don't hear them but you always do and you always get juiced no matter what they say. You want to prove something to them even though you know that they don't really care about you. All they're doing is worrying about their bets and reliving at your expense what they did and didn't do when they were your age and had the chance. It's kind of pitiful really but there they are, hearkening at the rail like the sad and jealous fools they are. I'd be real surprised if it wasn't one of them who has been calling me on the phone. They'll be on everybody's case big time tonight. And Okie, who never played a down in his life, will be the loudest of them all.

KOYL carries *Roughneck Football* live on Friday nights and runs the replays at eight every Saturday morning during the season. Maddox and Crews do a call-in show on Mondays after practice. Dees is not involved in that. Except for Sunday mornings, when a church service is aired, the rest of the time is devoted to country music and tons of commercials. I haven't heard but I guess they'll run the replay of the state game next Saturday.

"Sugar?" Mr. Shack says.

He knows better.

"Just coffee," I say.

I hang my coat on the stand beside the door to the garage and take down my coveralls. I step into them, add my arms, zip the zipper, and pat the breast pocket out of habit. It's not empty, which puzzles me. Mr. Shackleford and I have never spoken about the perk but I feel a need to say something this time. I pull the bill out.

"What's this for?" I say.

"A token of my confidence in you, Young Cody,"

Mr. Shack says. "I'd just as soon not have to ask for it back though. If you know what I mean."

"I do," I say. "Thanks, Mr. Shack. These tens come in handy."

I slip the bill into my wallet.

"I'm sure they do," Mr. Shack says. "Just don't tell the Athletic Association. They might dig up a rule we don't know about."

"Tell them what?" I say.

Mr. Shack grins a gummy grin.

"Thanks again," I say.

"Point's made, Young Cody," Mr. Shack says. "Quit thanking me. The pleasure's mine."

Roughneck Football is on the air. Oak Grove has kicked off into the end zone and the ball has been spotted at the twenty. I listen to Maddox:

"...up in an I-right formation. Porter splits to the near or left side. They call him Beep-Beep and he can fly. The Roughnecks will be working from right to left on your dial during these first twelve minutes. Stills eyes that big Oak Grove defense. We'll set them for you in just a moment. Here we go. Stills is down and under his center now. He takes the snap, turns, gives to Beene straight ahead. Holy Moses! Welcome to the playoffs, Mr. Beene. That's Chad Adler of the Tigers coming through to make the stop at the line. He may even have pushed him back a yard..."

"Somebody missed his man," Mr. Shackleford says. "Course we won't mention any names."

He hands me my cup. I blow on the steaming coffee and nod. I lost my footing when I hiked the ball and the noseman crabbed past me with a minimum of resistance. Beene, our sophomore fullback, took the handoff unprotected and my guy racked up an unassisted tackle. It was his first and last of the game. I wore him out after that, but Crews didn't pardon me for the opening play when we watched the tape the following Monday. He ran it back and forth—me slipping and the nose sliding by every time—and lectured at length on the disadvantage of trying to play the game of football from the prone position. Make a mistake on Friday night and Crews won't bother you about it. But he will read you the riot act come Monday afternoon. He'll let you know about it. Reviewing game videos with him can be a real ordeal. It's amazing what he sees. Little things. Fundamentals. Football is not an art to him. It's an exact science.

One thing about Mr. Shackleford, by the way: He doesn't miss much that happens in a game either and he doesn't miss anything that happens up front. He played in the line way back in the days of baggy pants, tight jerseys, and tiny shoulder pads. It was one-platoon ball and headgear was optional. He showed me a picture of himself dressed out and in it he looked like he'd be more than happy to remove your gizzard with his bare hands. He claims that he refused to wear a hat even when he had stitches in his head one time. He says that guys were tougher back then. I'm not sure about tougher. Crazier maybe. No way I'd go without a hat.

Maddox is reading the names of Oak Grove's defenders when Big Daddy enters the office. He's wiping Go-Jo off his hands with a red rag. I've been knowing "Big Daddy" Yelvingston for a long time now, but whenever I first see him after I haven't for a few days I always have to take a moment and just marvel. *Big* doesn't do him any kind of justice. *Massive* comes closer. *Vast* may be better than that. He's six five, more solid than not at 260, and bald as a cartop. Vast Daddy. You see him coming and hope he's on your side. He makes you feel like you've shrunk.

"Doc Ware say hose it off too?" Big Daddy says.

His voice is deep but it's softer than you'd think.

Mr. Shack says, "Did," and I say, "Hey," at the same time.

Big Daddy lays his rag on the Coke machine, which is level with his shoulders.

"How it feel to have your face in the morning paper and be a celebrity, Travis?" he says.

"More weird than anything else," I say.

"Don't be making him feel too important, Shirley," Mr. Shack says.

Mr. Shackleford is the only person I know who calls Big Daddy by his given name. Everybody else is either afraid to or doesn't think that Shirley fits. Both camps have a sound argument.

"Boy can't afford to wear no swole-up head today," Big Daddy says. "Do and old Grooms'll hang it on the wall for him tonight. Ain't that right, Travis?"

"Might anyway," I say.

Big Daddy laughs his great booming laugh. His voice may be softer than you'd expect but his laugh isn't. It will startle you.

"Might if you don't watch him close," Big Daddy says. "Might indeed."

He opens the door.

"Come move this Caddy over for me, Travis," he says. "Time for us working mens to get busy."

"I'm on my way," I say.

I finish my coffee then take a red rag from the stack on the counter. I tie it on pirate-style, adjust my bill cap over it, and linger to hear my first punt.

Maddox: "...hit it at about the thirty-eight..."

Mr. Shack: "Maybe."

Maddox: "...low snap. He's got it. Steps. Kicks. It's a nice one. High and spiraling, turning over. There won't be any return on this. Martin lets it go and it's rolling. It's going to die at about the seventeen. So. Oil Camp was able to get one first down..."

Me: "I didn't miss that ball, Mr. Shack."

Once in a while I remind him of this fact just to let him have the pleasure of seeing that he has succeeded in getting a rise out of me.

"Calm down, Young Cody," Mr. Shack says. "Tell me something. Did old Lunker have him a souvenir on the hiney where you smacked him last week?"

"Sure did," I say.

Lunk's bruise didn't start giving up and turning yellow until Wednesday. It was still pretty painful-looking yesterday.

"A once-in-a-lifetime play," Mr. Shack says.

"Once too many," I say.

I back Dr. Ware's freshly tuned Cadillac out of the garage and ease it into the wash bay. Big Daddy motions me up with hands that are the size and color of baseball gloves. The DeVille is absolutely hushed inside. The seat is like a good sofa. It's plenty firm but not hard. I've only driven this car to and from the

Wares' house and around the station but I would dearly love to know how it handles on the open road. It has power everything, including headlamps that come on by themselves and dim down when necessary. All you have to do is steer it and try to stay awake. It's like a rolling living room.

"So," I say. "I guess you'll be there tonight."

"Plans to," Big Daddy says.

I wait to see if he's going to elaborate but it's obvious that he's not. He just ties on his rubber apron and starts swabbing the tires of the Cadillac with a soapy brush. The bell sounds before I can come up with a better lead.

"Pull the door to on your way out," he says.

"Big Daddy" Yelvingston has got his own place and he occupies it. He doesn't invite you into it often. He grew up in Oil Camp and played his ball before integration. He was All-Everything at Woodland, the old black school. Mr. Shack told me that he got his nickname when a coach from Jonesboro said that he was going to be the next "Big Daddy" Lipscomb, who was a star tackle for the Baltimore Colts during the fifties. But our Big Daddy didn't make the pros. He went to Grambling for a year, then he quit school, joined the army, and was among the first American troops in Vietnam. I tried to get him to talk about 'Nam one time and he made it clear that whatever he saw and did over there is strictly off-limits.

"War nasty, Travis," he said. "Nasty and foolish. Best to set it aside you ask me. I start my forgetting on the plane home. Ain't a easy thing to do. I hope you never haves to see it. OK?"

"OK," I said.

I like Big Daddy a lot even though I don't really know him. He reminds me of Crews. Both of them are as good as anybody at what they do and both of them have a knack of making you want their approval. You try to do everything right when they're around. You get the feeling that they've eliminated mistakes themselves and that you'd do well to imitate them. It's a high standard but you work hard to hack it because they don't give you any other choice.

For the next couple of hours I'm so busy filling tanks, wiping windshields, checking oil, and vacuuming floorboards that I only get to hear a down or two of the playoff tapes when I go inside to make change or run a credit card through the deal. The quarterfinal game with Vidalia is on right now. It was the most intense of the three. We never trailed Oak Grove or South Cameron, but Vidalia hit a long pass for an early touchdown, threatened but stalled late in the second period, and had us down 7–0 at halftime.

We came out and immediately turned it around with two big plays. Beep-Beep returned the second-half kickoff all the way, then the Vikings fumbled deep on their first possession. Halliburton made the stick, I recovered for us at the eleven, and we punched it across on third-and-one from the two. That ended the scoring. We just slugged it out between the thirties with them from there on in.

I had my best statistical game of the year that night: four solo tackles, twelve assists, two sacks, and the turnover on defense, three pancakes, and zero un-assisted stops allowed on offense. I even punted better than usual: seven times, forty-two yards a try. Crews graded me out at 93. My average is 86. I wouldn't mind just sitting down and listening to that one again, but things are hopping at Shackleford's Texaco this morning.

This is good and bad. It's good because I like being occupied. It's bad because literally everybody I have waited on so far today has brought tonight up. I knew this was going to happen and I didn't mind it for a little while, but then it started getting on my nerves and making me dread hearing the bell. I wish there was some way that without sounding rude or ungrateful I could let everybody know that I'd just as soon answer questions about something other than how I feel and what I think will happen tonight. A few minutes ago this man I didn't even know shook my hand and told me that he'd been having trouble sleeping all week.

"I keep waking up thinking, What if we lose?" he said. "I don't believe I could stand it."

I'm sure that he meant well but all it did was make me start worrying about the external pressure that's on us tonight. As if we won't be putting enough of it on ourselves, a lot of people just like that man—people who are complete strangers to me—will base how they feel about themselves and their town for a long time on the outcome of this ball game. They have a symbolic stake in it too and they want us to represent them well, which means that they want us not just to play hard but to win. Effort doesn't mean anything to them. They take that for granted. Victory is the only success they understand and even though I'm just as guilty of it as anybody, I am beginning to think that maybe we've got ourselves a screwed-up set of priorities around here. Nobody, myself included, seems to be excited about the simple fact that we're in the finals for the first time in five years. We ought to be celebrating that instead of wondering what we'll do if we lose. Winning makes people weird after a while. They forget the point of competition, which is to do the best that you can.

Every now and then I reach for my toes to test my back. The longer I'm up and moving the better it feels. I bend, extend my arms for a five-count, then stand. I'm on number six of a set of ten when somebody turns into the station leaning on his horn obnoxiously. I'm ready with a menacing glare, but when I see who it is I only wave dismissively and shake my head. It's Lunk in his daddy's pickup and there's a field-dressed buck in the bed. I grin. I always grin when the Lunker shows up because he's just that kind of a guy. He pulls me out of myself, which is exactly what I need right now.

"Behold the spoils of the hunt, T," Lunk says as he steps out of the truck.

He leaves the engine running.

"Must be nice to have the day off," I say.

"Must be nice to have some spending money," Lunk says.

I lick an index finger and describe a vertical line in the air.

"Score one for the captain," I say.

We admire the slain deer. He's a beauty with a fine rack of eight points. Unlike Lunk I'm saddened to see him dead. I'm no hunter. Lunk is and always has been.

I notice that along with the tag, he stuck the newspaper picture of Grooms onto one of the points.

"Nice touch," I say.

"Thought you'd appreciate a little voodoo to go along with all the other stuff you do," Lunk says. "He was in the paper this morning with two dudes I would have swore were movie stars at first. Then I took a closer look and saw that they was just us."

"I bet most people made that same mistake," I say. "Where'd you get him?"

"Somewhere you'll never go," Lunk says. "How anybody could grow up with Pawpaw for a grandfather, Glen for a brother, and me for a main home and not be normal about hunting is beyond me."

"Just lucky, I guess," I say.

Not that they all didn't try, especially Pawpaw, who hunted anything that moved and had a fur. He thought it was a way of life, a necessary thing. I never could quite see it though. I'd rather fish. Pawpaw used to tell me that it was the same difference, but fishing always seemed more sporting to me than hiding in a tree and blowing away something vulnerable and warm-blooded that just happened to wander into the wrong place at the wrong time. I shot a few birds and squirrels and rabbits, but I felt awful about it every time and finally just gave it up. I never killed a deer. I had a chance to one time though. A big old buck was standing directly in front of me but instead of smoking him, I picked up a stick and threw it at him to scare him off. He was that close. The way he bounded away and disappeared into the woods was one of the most thrilling things I've ever seen.

"Maybe we ought to check your genealogy," Pawpaw said when I told him what I'd done. "I'm not sure everything's on the up and up here, Travis."

I don't see it as a defect myself. I never cared for the taste of venison anyway.

"Well, lookee here," Mr. Shack says, approaching the pickup. "How many's this make for you, Lunker?"

"Lost count, Mr. Shackleford," Lunk says. "Several. I've been knocking down my limit every season for a long time now."

"I could use some meat if y'all have any extra," Mr. Shack says. "I'm getting a little feeble to go stomping through the forest much these days."

"That's one reason I dropped by," Lunk says. "Naturally I had to show the Great White Hunter here how I spent my morning but Daddy also wanted me to come see if you'd be willing to cook up a mess of your chili for the team during the break."

"A little Christmas feed from the Touchdown Club?" Mr. Shack says. "You tell your daddy I said I'd be proud to."

"I don't know who all's going to be in town while we're off but we'll set up a night for whoever is," Lunk says.

I realize that I've been so preoccupied with the game for the past few days that I completely forgot about Christmas being next Friday. We'll be out of school for two weeks starting Wednesday. I need to buy presents for Nita, Mom, Glen, and Lunk. I guess I'll make a Christmas Eve run on Thursday.

"Anytime's fine with me," Mr. Shack says. "Looks like we got a fair start on the main ingredient here."

"Don't worry about that," Lunk says. "Daddy said tell you all you need to do is bring your magic spoon. We've got plenty of venison in the freezer already and he'll take care of everything else with Touchdown Club money."

"Tell him he can just schedule a cheeseburger for me," I say.

"Wuss," Lunk says. "I never heard of anybody not liking venison. It's un-American. Listen to this, y'all. I thought they was going in for sure right here."

He reaches into the truck and turns up the radio. It's tuned to KOYL.

Maddox: "...spotted just shy of the Roughneck fifteen. Fourth- and—let's call it three. Here come the Vikings. We're less than two minutes before halftime and the clock's running. One fifty-six, fifty-five, fifty-four. Vidalia leads by a touchdown and is looking for more."

Dees: "You have to think they might just try to draw Oil Camp offsides then call time if that doesn't work. This is chip-shot field-goal territory."

Maddox: "We'll see. Johnson sets them in a slot to the right side. LaCoss is the slotback, Hagan the split end. Johnson wants Hagan to take a wider split. He waves him out. Now he's satisfied. He goes under for the snap. Long count. This could be a hoax. But no. It's for real. Johnson has the ball and the lines are engaged. Johnson's dropping straight back. He gives to Morrison the fullback on a little delay. Holy Moses! Folks, I am here to tell you that there is nowhere for the runner to hide or go thanks to Travis Cody."

Dees: "Remember that one."

Maddox: "Yes indeed. The play never had a chance to develop. Cody met the ballcarrier a yard behind the line and drove him all the way back to the twenty..."

"Shut the boy down is what I'm talking about," Lunk says. "Great job, T. Very big. Very big stick."

He raises his arms and we high-five in retrospect.

"Not much of a call," Mr. Shack says. "Nothing against your fine tackle, Young Cody, but that one was misguided. He said it was a delay but that was a pure draw if I remember right and I've about decided a draw's the worst play in football. Stay at the house and deal with your blocker and it'll never work, which you proved. Now. What I really want to know is if y'all plan to run that special punt you two boys unveiled for us last week."

"I'd bet against it myself," Lunk says. "My butt's not ready for another one of those. It still has the imprint of a ball on it."

"Just checking," Mr. Shack says.

"He's never going to let us live that one down, Lunk," I say.

"That's all right," Lunk says. "I probably wouldn't let us either if I was somebody else."

Mr. Shack puts a hand on Lunk's shoulder.

"What's the word, Lunker?" he says.

"I believe we'll take them, Mr. Shackleford," Lunk says. "I really do."

He thumps the impaled image of Grooms and looks at me.

"Our famous friend right here's going to have his major college hands full," he says. "That I know."

84

The telephone bell above the office door begins to ring insistently.

"Keep your britches on," Mr. Shack says. "I hope you're right, Lunker. Tell your daddy I said give me a call about that feed. Maybe we'll just celebrate ourselves a championship. All my best to you for tonight."

"Will do," Lunk says. "Thanks."

We watch Mr. Shack stride away.

"How you feeling?" Lunk says.

"You want the truth?" I say.

"Nothing but," Lunk says.

"I'm getting seriously tired of people asking me how I feel and what's going to happen tonight, man," I say. "Nervous as hell is how I feel. What's going to happen is anybody's guess."

"Mind if I take one?" Lunk says.

"Might as well," I say.

"You're going to have a good one, T. Time you get through with Grooms he'll be in about as bad a shape as this deer."

I glance at the buck. His throat is slashed and his blue tongue is hanging out one side of his mouth.

"Don't get carried away," I say.

"I'm not," Lunk says. "I'm just telling you what I saw in a vision out on the stand this morning."

"You must've been hallucinating then."

"Bull hockey. Know what Modisette came up and told me after practice Wednesday?"

Matt Modisette is our scout team center and noseguard. He imitated Grooms for me all week.

"No telling," I say.

"He said he felt sorry for Grooms," Lunk says.

"No joke. He said, 'Cody's on a mission, man.' He said he'd never seen you hit like you hit Wednesday."

I did have a good practice Wednesday, maybe my best one ever. I guess the letter I got from Coach Tinsley the day before inspired me. For a moment I consider telling Lunk about it, then I decide against that. Keeping the scholarship possibility a secret seems like a better idea.

"You're just stroking me," I say.

"I kid you not, home," Lunk says. "Modisette wasn't the only one who noticed it either. We all did. You were a maniac out there. Stills said you gave him sore hands snapping the ball so hard. Shoot. You even had Crews and Wroten smiling during goal line."

"Now I know you're lying," I say. "They don't know how to smile."

"Think what you want," Lunk says. "I've been watching you close and the fact is this, T: Jericho Grooms is yours for the taking, don't matter how many colleges want his ass. You're ready."

"Enough," I say. "I might start believing this noise."

"Believe it," Lunk says. "You own that bastard."

Lunk and I play side by side. He's our left guard on O and our strong guard on D. He'll have three stripes under the football on the letter jacket he gets at the banquet next spring. I'll only have two on mine but I'm not jealous of Lunk. I'm proud of him. He's my blood brother but he seems as much like my real one as Glen does because we grew up together and because we've always been there for each other. We pick each other up when one of us needs it and we always sense when that is. I don't know if all of what he just said was really true but that doesn't matter. What does matter is the message of confidence. That part was as honest as the blood we drew from ourselves with a kitchen knife when we were nine years old. We sliced our thumbs, pressed them together, and adopted each other. We swore lifetime loyalty.

"Well, I guess I better load and road and let you get on back to the grind," Lunk says. "Blow that nervous crap off while you're at it, man. OK? Loosen up."

"I'm trying," I say. "What're you doing until the pep rally?"

"First I'm skinning Bambi here and then I'm taking him to the locker plant. After that I don't know. I'll probably eat something then go over to Beep's for a little eight-ball in the basement."

"Tell him not to forget his comb this afternoon," I say. "Somebody might want to borrow it."

"What if he decides not to loan it?"

"Fists will fly," I say.

"You and your rituals," Lunk says. "Get a life, T. I'm out of here."

We shake hands in three quick motions, catching each other's fingers and holding tight for a moment at the end.

8

Beep-Beep and Halliburton are the only ones from the lineup with me in third-hour study hall. We started out sitting together at a table back by the newspaper and magazine racks but Mrs. Richardson pulled the plug on that arrangement less than a week into the semester, which was fine with me because I usually have homework to finish or reading to do and third period gives me the chance. Except for a terminal C in whatever math I'm taking, my grades have always been pretty good. Keeping them that way is important to me. Sooner or later I'll need them for college. I knew I was going to have to get away from Beep-Beep and Halliburton before the first day was over. My average wouldn't have survived their bad habits. All they wanted to do was tell jokes, play table football, and horse around. Those are strong arguments against doing homework no matter how much you have.

"Yo, Beep," Halliburton said on the day Mrs. Richardson called our hand.

"Yo, Burt," Beep said.

He was folding a piece of yellow tablet paper into a thumpable triangle.

"You seen Ray Charles's new piano yet?" Halliburton said.

"Never have," Beep said.

"Ray ain't neither," Halliburton said.

For some reason that tickled Beep unduly, which set Halliburton and me off too. We got to snorting and giggling, and trying not to only made it worse. I thought I was going to suffocate.

"You boys," Mrs. Richardson said.

She was moving toward us. Halliburton recovered enough to speak but Beep and I were still losing it.

"Ma'am?" Halliburton said.

Mrs. Richardson was leaning on our table, supporting her mass with her knuckles. Her glasses swung from a chain around her thick neck.

"What's going on back here?" she said.

"Not much," Halliburton said. "We just be grooving."

Beep made a noise in the back of his mouth. I had to fight off another wave of hysterics.

"Just grooving?" Mrs. Richardson said.

"That's about all," Halliburton said.

He was pushing our luck for us.

"I see," Mrs. Richardson said. "Well, you're going to groove yourselves right on out the door if we don't make a change here. Travis, you remain seated. You others, I want y'all there and there."

She pointed to tables on opposite sides of the library.

"Enough of these monkeyshines," she said.

Mrs. Richardson didn't know it because I didn't say it out loud but I was thanking her over and over as I watched Beep and Burt shuffle to their new places. She'd just saved me from wasting any more time. I'd already wasted enough.

Homework has to wait on game Fridays though. Even if I have a big test I always start my Friday study hall by reading the preview story in the Shreveport paper. I read it, freak for a minute, then try to forget it, which is a two-out-of-three proposition. I have the reading and freaking down to absolutes but the forgetting needs some work. It's almost ten-thirty, time to give it a shot. If this were Friday the third-period tardy bell would have sounded twenty-five minutes ago. I head for the office.

Mr. Shackleford is holding a pamphlet and looking at the Bunn-O-Matic. The South Cameron replay is on the radio, first quarter. We've already scored.

"You bring the Sports?" I say.

"Left it in my car," Mr. Shack says. "Answer me this, Young Cody. What would you do if the instructions for your new coffeepot directed you to clean it with vinegar?"

"Probably run some vinegar through it."

"I was afraid you might say that. Sounds awful queer to me but I need to do something. Coffee's tasting like it has metal in it this morning. You notice that?"

"I don't guess I did," I say. "Really vinegar?"

"What it says here in the book."

"Can't hurt to try it then," I say. "I'm taking a break."

"From what?" Mr. Shack says.

"From my SSA duties."

"Oh," Mr. Shack says. "How long you planning on staying? One of us needs to go out and jump Mrs. Hammontree's car, Lord help us all, before you leave. That was her on the line a while ago."

"I was thinking I'd go at noon so I can eat but I'll drive out and take care of her," I say.

Mr. Shack glances at his watch.

"Shouldn't put you much past twelve," he says. "I'd hate it if you ran into a problem and got yourself bogged down out there though."

"I won't," I say. "I can pick up a bite on the way back. You shutting down for the rally?"

"Wouldn't miss it. We're locking the doors from two to three. Everybody in town is, from what I hear. We're coming over to adore y'all. Undoubtedly you saw the item in the Wiper."

"Did," I say.

The *Oil Camp News* carried a full-page ad in it this week with a picture of the team below a banner headline that said GO ROUGHNECKS! TAKE STATE! It was sponsored by the Downtown Merchants, who announced elsewhere in the paper that they'd be closing their stores for an hour today so that everybody who wanted to could attend the pep rally.

"Go ahead and take you a few minutes," Mr. Shack says. "Me and Shirley'll cover the front."

"I won't be long," I say.

It has been warming up steadily since I rode over to the stadium this morning. It's nice out here. I sit in the backseat of Mr. Shackleford's Impala and leave the door open while I read what my favorite journalist has typed up about tonight's game.

Rivalry Renewed for Title Tilt
By Nick Van Noate
Staff Writer

A 12-mile stretch of blacktop separates the towns of Pineview and Oil Camp, communities that grew up together after the discovery of black gold in the piney woods of northwest Louisiana.

The boom days are long since over, but the rivalry that has existed between these two small towns from the beginning is still very much alive.

Each November that rivalry reaches its annual peak on the gridiron. Perhaps more than anywhere else in the state, football is an integral part of life there, and teams from Pineview and Oil Camp have been playing it against each other for as long as anybody in either town can remember.

Traditionally the final game of the regular season, more often than not the Pineview–Oil Camp get-together, takes place with a district title on the line. Tonight, however, the sometimes bitter, always entertaining feud will be renewed at considerably higher stakes as the 13–0 Pelicans and the 12–1 Roughnecks clash for the Class AA state championship at Roughneck Field.

Kickoff time is 7:30 p.m.

Oil Camp and Pineview have won or shared all but two of the District 1 AA crowns contested during the spectacular tenures of their present head coaches. Oil Camp's J. C. Crews owns a remarkable overall record of 229–61–4, including five state titles, while Pineview's Charlie Webb has posted a 172–56–1 mark. Webb has guided two Pineview clubs to the state finals, but neither was able to capture the championship flag.

Oil Camp enjoys a 51–27 edge in the series.

A single point decided this year's regular season meeting at Pineview as the Pelicans turned back a late two-point attempt by Oil Camp to preserve a 7–6 victory on Nov. 20.

"We were lucky," Webb told a caller Friday afternoon. "Of course, you always have to consider yourself lucky when you beat the Camp."

Pineview used nearly eight minutes of the second period in driving 82 yards for what proved to be the winning touchdown. It was the longest sustained march against the Oil Camp defense all season.

"I've watched the tape of that one more times than I care to admit," said Crews, who was speaking on his office phone Friday morning. "They executed perfectly on every play, and we just had a letdown. I don't know which was the cause and which was the result, but nobody moved the football on us like that before or since. They had 149 yards of offense, total, and 82 of them came on that one drive."

"It was our best offensive effort of the year," Webb said. "We've looked as good in other games, but you have to rate what you do according to who you do it against, and Oil Camp is far and away the best team we've faced."

The Roughnecks, who advanced the ball consistently throughout the game but twice stopped themselves by fumbling inside the Pelican

20, finally scored with just over two minutes remaining. Crews elected to go for the win.

"I thought we had too much momentum at that point not to," Crews said. "Given the same circumstances, I wouldn't hesitate to do it again. It just didn't work out for us the other night."

While few observers condemned Crews's decision to try for two, which almost certainly would have given Oil Camp the victory, many did question his calling a run instead of a pass on the conversion attempt.

"That's a long three yards," Webb said. "We were surprised that they tried to run on us down there, especially up the middle. Well, everybody but our noseman was. He read the thing and made a heads-up play, a great play."

Indeed he did. Pineview noseguard Jericho Grooms, a senior move-in from Lufkin, Texas, who began drawing the interest of major college scouts as a sophomore, blew past Oil Camp center Travis Cody and stopped Roughneck fullback Scott Beene in the backfield. The Pelicans ran two plays after the kickoff, then picked up the game's most important first down, forced Oil Camp to use its last time-out, and ran out the clock by downing the ball three times in a row.

Did Crews consider passing?

"You consider everything in a situation like that," Crews said. "But we knew they'd be looking for a pass, and we'd been fairly successful leaving the Belly option with the fullback, so we decided to go with that. It was a called play that time though, not an option. In retrospect I think the only mistake we made was in handcuffing our quarterback [senior Jody Stills]. He might have been able to make something happen if we'd left him alone. But Grooms got in there so fast that I don't know."

What about an onside kick?

"Never entered my mind," Crews said. "Even though we missed the conversion and only had one time-out left, I thought our best bet was to kick deep, pin them, force a punt and take our last shot. Unfortunately, we let them convert on third down and never got the football back."

Pineview's road to the final round included victories over Many (33–0), Notre Dame Crowley (26–6) and Zachary (19–7). Oil Camp defeated Oak Grove (28–0), Vidalia (14–7) and South Cameron (21–2).

Grooms, a certain All-State selection whose name has appeared on several national blue-chip lists this year, anchors both sides of the line for the Pelicans.

"Jericho Grooms is probably as good a high school lineman as there is in the state," Crews said. "He blocks like a train, and he tackles like a bear trap. We had a kid [Cody] going one-on-one with him four weeks ago, and we dealt with him very well for the most part. But he made the big play for them when they had to have it."

As in the previous game, Oil Camp's Cody has the unenviable assignment of working head-to-head against Grooms again tonight.

"Cody handled him better than anybody has all year," Webb said. "But Jericho will get his pops in. He's always going to be a factor."

In addition to Grooms, tonight's contest will showcase three other players who are strong candidates for All-State honors: halfback Gregory

Washington and lineman Ramsey Godchaux of Pineview, and lineman Nathan Bass of Oil Camp.

A complete list of probable starters is in today's Scoreboard section.

Not surprisingly, both coaches are taking the "dance with what brung you" approach to the encounter, which means that fancy tricks will play second fiddle to basic, smash-mouth football from two teams that mirror each other in almost every way. Both will work chiefly out of an I-formation on offense and both will present a five-man front with two linebackers, a rover and three deepbacks on defense.

"We may have a wrinkle or two they haven't seen," Crews said. "But no, we haven't changed anything."

"Block and tackle," Webb said. "That's what we do, that's what they do, and that's what you'll see 48 minutes of this time. It's ball-control, ground-oriented football. You always keep an ace up your sleeve for emergencies, but there's no reason to break out a whole new deck at this late stage."

Will revenge be a motivator for the Roughnecks?

"We haven't mentioned it," Crews said. "I won't deny that we think we have something to prove to the Pelicans, but first and foremost we're playing to win the state championship. That's our number-one priority. Beating Pineview for the sake of beating Pineview is secondary."

"You don't need revenge to motivate yourself for a ball game like this," Webb said. "You don't even need a rivalry. This is for all the jewels. I honestly think that both teams would be just as up for Happy Hearts Elementary as they will for each other.''

Anyone who detects a note of sincerity in either of those last two comments is advised to get in touch with Crews and Webb immediately. They have some nice beachfront condominiums for sale up near the Arkansas border.

Bottom line? Forget the stakes. High as they are, they don't mean nearly as much as this: Pineview vs. Oil Camp.

These are the best of enemies.

Hats off to old Nick. He rose to the occasion at the end there and told it like it is. My guts are churning and my palms are damp with nervous sweat. Seeing the situation laid out in print, I'm beyond freaked. I couldn't study right now for a suitcase full of large bills. If I were in third period I'd have to ask Mrs. Richardson to write me a hall pass so I could go to the rest room and puke.

"You boys," she'd probably say. "You get far too worked up over a simple game."

In another place she might be right. This isn't a simple game here though. This is way more than that. I can see it in people's eyes this morning. I can see them thinking: This is Pineview vs. Oil Camp, Cody, and your assignment is the featured attraction.

I skip the lineups, fold the paper, and lay it on the seat. The pictures of Grooms, Lunk, and me are facing up. I stare at Grooms for a moment, then at Lunk, then at myself. Today we're the top story. Tomorrow we'll be lining the bottoms of trash cans or used to start fires. We may already be. Some people who got this paper won't even look at the Sports section. They'll ignore it the way I ignore the Classifieds.

I wonder what percentage of the total number of people who see the paper today will read all or part of Van Noate's story. In Oil Camp and Pineview it's undoubtedly close to 100 percent. But what about all of the others? How many of them will read it? Probably not too many. Probably not enough to come anywhere near the majority. I actually kind of like that idea. I like it even more when I take it to the next level, which is to think that of all people everywhere only a tiny fraction of them are aware that this is taking place. It's really not that big when you look at it in relation to the overall human picture. Everything that can happen to people will happen again today, same as usual. Birth and death, marriage and divorce, war and peace, victory and defeat. All of it is happening this morning while I'm sitting here, it'll be happening tonight while I'm having my battle with Grooms, and it'll keep on happening in the future while I'm rotting in the ground. I mean, the world doesn't revolve around a Pineview–Oil Camp game. It just seems to. And even then it's only for a little while. I need to keep this in mind.

Nita shows up shortly after I finish my break. She's driving her mother's Lexus and she's looking like a model in a black sweater over a white turtleneck. She's also wearing my Senior Key. We didn't do anything last night except talk on the phone so I haven't seen her since yesterday at school. The sight causes my heartbeat to jump up a notch. She wants to know if I can fill her up. I give her a quick kiss and tell her that the same question has entered my head more times than I can count during the past few months. I put in subtle and not-so-subtle plugs for my cause every chance I get. What I really wish is that we could just cut our thumbs, press them together, and get the final frontier of our relationship over with. It doesn't work that way though. It's not that simple.

"Why do guys have such one-track minds?" Nita says.

"Because of girls like you," I say.

Nita draws the corners of her mouth back, halfway smirking and halfway smiling. Her brown hair is pulled away from her face. Plastic barrettes hold it in place and it shines like it's wet. A trace of Calvin Klein's Eternity perfume is in evidence. The way she looks and smells makes me breathe different.

"Just give me some gasoline, Cody," she says. "I have a big date tonight."

"Me too," I say. "Who's yours with?"

I rest my elbows on the door of the Lexus and make an issue of inhaling the delicate scent of Eternity on Nita Tyler. I'm relieved to be thinking about something besides football for a minute. Nita reaches out and yanks the bill of my cap down over my eyes.

"Somebody who doesn't have a car of his own to take me in," she says.

I leave my eyes covered.

"I can still smell you," I say. "It's a nice fragrance too. Know what?"

"What?" she says.

"I don't believe I'd mind going blind if the last thing I ever saw was you," I say.

"What a sweet thing to say," she says.

Easy points. I push my cap back into place.

"I had a dream you were in," I say.

"I'm almost afraid to ask for details," she says.

"Don't be. It was just you out at the lake."

"Were you there?" she says.

"I imagine so since I was watching you."

"What was I doing? Nothing obscene I hope."

"Just running along the bank."

"How exciting."

"Depends on your point of view."

Nita smiles, which makes the chicken-pox scar on her left cheek crease oblong. I always think that I have her face memorized and then I see her and realize that I don't. You can't keep something that well made in your mind. It's too much of a masterpiece to hold in that way. Even pictures of her miss most of it. The one in my wallet is only a hint. You have to see it live to appreciate it. What a pretty face she has. Everything goes with everything else. And she wears only a touch of makeup. I guess she knows that more would be an insult.

"Saw you in the paper," she says. "I already put it on my mirror."

"Pretty slick," I say.

"Were you surprised?" she says.

"Totally."

"Me too. I screamed."

"Scared you that bad, did it?"

"Gas, Cody," she says. "I've got some shopping to do before the pep meeting."

"Think you can cover all of downtown Camp by then?" I say. "It ought to take you at least thirty minutes."

"Just come on," she says.

I go set the pump, then return to the open window.

"Lunk killed him a deer this morning," I say.

"Gross," Nita says. "I don't see how anybody could just shoot an innocent deer."

"Me either, really," I say. "It's manly man stuff and I'm an honorary sissy. Oil?"

"You are not," she says. "Sissies don't play football last I heard. They don't ride motorcycles or work at filling stations either, so just shut up. Check it if you want to."

"Undo the latch," I say.

Nita pops the hood. I lift it, prop it open, pull the dipstick, wipe it, reinsert it, and take it back out.

"This is brand-new," I say.

"I didn't say you had to check it, motorhead," Nita says. "What're we doing after the game?"

I drop the hood.

"I haven't thought that far ahead," I say. "What do you want to do?"

I begin to wash the windshield.

"If we win I want to go to Shreveport and get something to eat," Nita says. "You pick the place. I'll drive and buy."

"But what if we don't?" I say. "What if Grooms munches on me from start to finish?"

"Then we'll probably just sit around and act like the world ended," she says. "Like last time."

"Can I change the subject?" I say.

"Good idea," she says.

"Hang on," I say.

I wipe the glass on the passenger side then trot around to catch the handle of the pump before it trips off. I stop the meter at seventeen even.

"Are y'all twirling this afternoon?" I say.

"Yep," Nita says. "We're doing 'La Bamba' again. I'm about sick of that routine too."

"Like I said, it all depends on your point of view. You owe us seventeen dollars."

Nita hands me a ten, a five, and two ones.

"Do I get to see you after the pep rally?" she says.

"Don't know. I won't have but a little while and I'll be starting to go crazy by then anyway. Not that I haven't already. Everybody and all their kids and grandkids and cats and dogs have been wanting to talk football this morning. Maybe I'll see you before."

"Poor Cody. Come here in case you don't."

I move closer and she holds my face with her cool hands. The smell of Eternity fills my nose as she gives me a long, slow kiss. Her tongue is wet and warm and it tastes pepperminty.

"Yum," I say.

"That's for luck," Nita says. "I'll keep my fingers and toes crossed for you too."

"You do that," I say. "What about your legs?"

"Hush," she says. "Come here again though."

She starts the Lexus.

"What?" I say.

"I want to whisper something," she says.

I put my hands on my knees and lean toward her. I look down at my Chuck Taylors.

"Are you nervous, Cody?"

I can feel the heat of her breath. I nod.

"I mean real nervous," she says.

I nod again.

"I thought so. Know how come?"

I shake my head. Nita's lips brush my ear.

"Because you're getting this huge pimple, dude," she says.

I just stand there with a wide and happy smile on my face as she drives away.

9

The station pickup is a 1965 Chevrolet that has never been washed, waxed, or parked in shelter overnight. Time, neglect, and the elements have combined to fade its color a shade lighter than the original blue. It's pretty beat-up too. Big Daddy keeps the engine singing a smooth song though, and that's all you want from a working truck. The outside doesn't matter. The only thing Big Daddy hasn't been able to straighten out since it started happening is that the gearshift will hang up on you every once in a while when you try to drop back into first after a stop. There's no pattern to it. You might go for a month without having it happen or you might have to deal with it half a dozen times in one day.

The shifter grabs on me at the light that governs the highway where it intersects with Main Street, which is decorated for the holiday season. The light stanchions are wrapped to look like candy canes and the power lines are strung with silver tinsel and colored bulbs. I don't know if it looks more pitiful at night when it's all lit up or during the day when it's not. Either way it's obvious that the heart has just about been cut out of this little business district. The Downtown Merchants are doing the best they can, but it's getting harder and harder for them to compete with Pineview's Wal-Mart and Shreveport's malls. Maybe half of the store windows still have displays in them. The rest are blank or boarded over.

I kill the engine, set the brake, and step out of the truck, noticing that Nita's mom's Lexus is parked on the corner opposite me, in front of the Rexall. My object here is to free the linkage, get back in, restart the engine, and be ready to roll before green. I don't make it. A couple of drivers behind me honk but they're just going to have to be patient.

"Let's go, Cody," somebody says. "You're holding up commerce."

It's Okie Colbert, Paul Maddox's old color man. He's on the sidewalk directly across the street and he's already half looped and slurring his words. Ignoring him, I work the jammed metal with my hands. Sometimes I have to use a screwdriver to pry this mess apart. At least it's a column and not a floor shifter, so I don't have to crawl under the truck.

"Shack needs him a Ford," Okie says. "They don't do that. Should I direct traffic?"

The linkage gives. I answer Okie by slamming the hood. The light is red again.

"You'll never catch Shack in a Ford," I say.

I jump back in the cab.

"That's just because he ain't drove one lately," Okie says. "Got my eye on you tonight, boy. Try not to blow it for us again if you don't mind."

Okie's voice and tone sound familiar. I realize why just as the light turns green. I peel out through the intersection, whip the truck into a parking spot beside the Sears catalog outlet, and slam on the brakes. I stop the engine and glance into the rearview mirror. Okie is moving unsteadily down the sidewalk. I leave the truck through the passenger door. Okie sees me and reverses his direction.

"Hey!" I say.

Okie doesn't acknowledge me.

"Hey, Okie!" I say.

He halts but doesn't turn. I trot up beside him and we walk around the corner together. The stores are on our left as we move along Main Street.

"I ought to kick your teeth in right here," I say.

I'm ready to do it too.

"What're you talking about, boy?" Okie says.

"You know exactly what I'm talking about unless you're drunker than I think," I say.

"I ain't but barely buzzed," Okie says.

"Whatever."

We reach the end of the row of stores and start across the First Baptist Church parking lot. This week the sign out front reads:

GOING TO HEAVEN?
FLIGHT TRAINING INSIDE

Okie suddenly stops. I move around so that I'm facing him. He's wearing about a week's worth of beard and his breath is straight bourbon. It's so strong that it's more like a taste than a smell. He fumbles around in the bib of his overalls in search of a cigarette, retrieves one, and tries to light it. But his hands are shaking so badly that he can't do it.

"Damnit," I say. "Here."

I take his lighter, ignite it, and hold the flame to his cigarette.

"Much obliged," he says.

"You been calling me on the telephone?" I say.

"I don't have no telephone to call you on," Okie says. "It's disconnected. Why would I call you anyway?"

"Have you, Okie?"

He gives himself away by smiling.

"Got you a little pissed off, did I?"

He exhales smoke through his nostrils.

"Yeah, you did," I say.

"Well, that's good," Okie says. "Because that's what you missing, boy. You could stand a little bit more pissed-off of a attitude out there."

"What difference does it make to you?" I say.

"A hundred bucks' worth. You let Grooms whip your young ass from hell to breakfast on that two-point call the other night and it cost me one hundred dollars."

"You made the bet, not me," I say.

"Yeah, Cody. And you lost it."

"I missed one block all night. One block. You think about that. And next time you have a problem with the way somebody plays ball maybe you ought to stay away from the telephone and go tell them about it to their face."

Okie sucks his cigarette and squints at me.

"Didn't I just?" he says.

"You wouldn't have though," I say.

"Tell you what, Cody," he says. "You can go ahead and do something about this or you can be on your merry way. I don't care which."

We're standing so close together that I don't even have to move my feet to get most of my weight behind the forearm I throw. It's only about three-quarter speed because I'm aware of my back, but the blow catches Okie flush on the chest and he goes down hard. I step on his dropped cigarette, then I watch him try to regain his breath. It takes him a while. When he finally does my first impulse is to apologize. I decide not to though.

He sits up, looks at me, and shakes his head.

"Didn't think you had the stones, Cody," he says.

"I got the stones, Okie," I say. "You all right?"

He nods.

"I'm calling us even then," I say.

"We'd tangle if I wasn't nine hundred years old, you know," he says.

"Must be my lucky day then," I say.

I start to walk away but Okie calls my name.

"What?" I say.

"That hard as you can hit?"

"Get a job, Okie," I say.

I wonder if anybody saw what just happened and hope not because even though he deserved it, Okie's nothing but a harmless clown and I'm not real proud of myself for forearming him. It wasn't the most brilliant move I've ever made. At least I finally know who was making those calls. I'm actually relieved that it was just Okie.

According to the rotating clock-thermometer above the Planters Bank and Trust it's forty-seven degrees at 11:04. I decide to stop at the Chowline on the way out to Mrs. Hammontree's instead of on the way back. I need something solid on my stomach. All I've had so far today is two cups of black coffee and that, coupled with my idiotic run-in with Okie, has left me feeling a little jangly, a little pissed off. Maybe this is a good thing. Maybe Okie is right after all.

The Chowline is half a mile out the highway. I raise an index finger off the wheel when people wave at me as I pass them. A few of them give me a power fist to let me know that they're with me and the rest of the Roughnecks all the way tonight. *Right,* I think. *If we win all of y'all still will be tomorrow. If not you won't. Simple as that.*

I'm almost an hour ahead of the noontime rush so I park and go inside instead of ordering at the drive-in window. I'll play a couple of numbers on the jukebox while I'm waiting for my food. The Chowline juke is loaded with oldies.

Some guys from a seismograph crew take up one of the three booths that line the left side of the small dining room. I'm guessing that they're seismographers because of their hair. All of them wear it extra long. They look like a band. Neither the two tables between the door and the counter is occupied. The pinball machine and the jukebox are on the right side of the room. The jukebox is silent but the pinball machine is ringing and buzzing in response to a ball being played by a junior high kid in a Metallica T-shirt and ripped jeans. He's flanked by two of his buds who are waiting their turns. I nod at them and they elbow each other.

"Y'all ready to kick Pineview's butt, Cody?" one of them says.

The one who's playing catches the ball on a flipper and they all three face me. I know what they want to hear.

"Damn straight," I say.

"Old Grooms is pretty bad, ain't he?" another one says.

"That's the word," I say.

I walk on up to the counter. I can see Mary Helen Clampit through the opening in the partition that separates the fountain area from the kitchen. She mouths the words "Just a sec."

I know what I want but I scan the menu anyway. The letters are white against a black background. They slide on and off. In the middle of the board, between the food side and the beverage side, is this message:

CONGRATULATIONS ROUGHNECK'S
ONE MORE TO GO
BEAT PINEVIEW

Mr. Parke pointed out to us once that the majority of Americans will use an apostrophe to form the plural of a word when they make a sign.

"Look around," he said. "You're surrounded by

unnecessary apostrophes. It's a crime against the mother tongue."

"Sorry, Travis," Mary Helen says. "I was making patties for the dinner crowd."

"No hurry," I say.

Mary Helen is Glen's age but she looks closer to mine. Her face is plain but I can see how it might grow on you. Glen dated her some when they were in high school but now they're just friends. Today she has on tan slacks and a white shirt with the top three buttons undone to show the thin gold chain that's around her neck. She's also wearing that brand of perfume that smells like dirt to me. I don't know what it's called but I do know that Nita would break my arm if she knew what it and Mary Helen's undone buttons are making me think.

"What can I get for you?" Mary Helen says. "A Number Three cheeseburger, a bag of onion rings, and a chocolate shake, I bet."

"You win," I say.

"How's your brother?" Mary Helen says.

"Fine. Working hard like everybody else."

"I hear you. Tell him I said hey."

"I'll do it," I say.

One of the seismographers walks up and begins drumming his fingers on the counter. His hair is in a ponytail that hangs between his shoulder blades. It hasn't been washed for a while. Judging from the way he smells, the rest of him hasn't either. Even if I do wind up in the patch for the next couple of years, I'll never let myself look as scuzzy as this guy does. He must have no pride at all.

"You want that order for here or to go?" Mary Helen says.

"To go," I say.

I move over to the jukebox and study titles. I fish a quarter out from among the change in my coveralls, slip it into the machine, and punch up three selections from my list. The Beatles are first with "Back in the U.S.S.R.," followed by the Rolling Stones with "Brown Sugar" and Tyrone Davis with "Turn Back the Hands of Time." That's a heavy-duty set. I take a seat at one of the tables. The sound of a jet airplane fills the room, the Beatles throw down some no frills rock 'n' roll, and Stills enters the Chowline like it's his cue. He's wearing a SKI LOUISIANA sweatshirt. The skier is a crawdad with shades on. Stills heads straight for the jukebox and stands in front of it with his eyes shut. The seismographers watch him like he's just landed from Mars but Stills is oblivious. He's gone with John, Paul, George, and Ringo.

"The Fab Four," he says when the tune ends. "Best there ever was."

He slaps my table as he heads for the counter to order and to flirt with Mary Helen. The Stones give him some raunchy accompaniment. Stills is the world's biggest flirt. A lot of guys don't like him because of that but I've always admired the easy way he handles himself around females myself. Stills will just walk up to one, whether he knows her or not, and talk to her like there's nothing to it at all. I could never do that. I don't have the nerve. Stills has an overdose of it. He even flirts with Mom when he comes over to the house, but I'm not offended. I just shake my head at him.

I look out the window. A big rig hauling pipe roars by. The seismographers file out and board their crew truck. They'll spend the rest of the day in the deep woods trying to find out what the earth has been up to for the past few million years. Then they'll get drunk, go to the game, and maybe look for a fight afterward. Oil-field trash. What a life. God, I hope I'm not living it this time next year.

A straw coated with Coke foam appears on my table.

"I-right, X open, Inside Belly Right Pass," Stills says.

"Sounds like a winner," I say. "Where have I heard it before?"

"We may score on the first play, Codysan," Stills says. "Quick six. Then all we'll have to do is play defense."

He pulls a chair out, turns it around, and sits on it backwards.

"What if we kick off?" I say.

"Won't happen. They always defer if they get the flip and we always take the ball. Pineview'll kick off. Haven't you read the tendency chart?"

"Too many times," I say. "But what if they get it and elect to receive just to give us something to think about?"

"Then we'll bust their nose three times, let Beep catch the punt, and score on whatever play the next one is. I'm into this call, man."

He shakes his cup.

"Me too," I say. "We really going right with it?"

"Unless I change my mind when we get out

there," Stills says. "I'm splitting Beep left no matter what though. He's usually been wide to the right when we've passed."

"Both times?" I say.

Stills smiles. We throw less than ten times a game because Crews is of the three-things-can-happen-and-two-of-them-are-bad school of passing. We'll pound you into next week with our running game but we pass about as often as Wroten laughs, which is why we're putting one up on our first play tonight. Pineview will be convinced that they're ready for anything but they won't really be ready for that pass. Their line will read our blocking scheme, think option, and come hard to the flow side. Their linebackers and rover will all move with the first fake, then commit and crash with the second because Beep will be the only receiver in the secondary. His job is to lull the cornerback who has him into thinking that they're not going to be involved, that Beep is just cruising along on a decoy route. Beep-Beep can leave anybody they put back there looking like he's waist-deep in water though, so it doesn't make much difference if the corner covers soft or not, or whether the safety picks him up once he makes his move. The race is over the moment Beep cuts and runs. That's the easy part. The hard part is giving Stills enough time to get the ball away.

We've spent about a third of our offensive work in practice this week on that one play. Crews has left the set and direction up to Stills and we've done it both ways from every formation we have even though we've known all along that we'll show a Power-I because that's our primary set and because the Pelicans will smell something funny if we come out in anything else. The play is just like a regular Inside Belly except that the split end turns up on a fly after slanting across and the backs have short patterns of their own after their fakes, just in case. The line, including the tight end, run blocks. It doesn't matter whether Beep is split left or right. The routes are the same. The fullback button-hooks at five after he gets up. He'll definitely get tackled on the first fake. The halfback does a quick sideline after the second fake. He'll probably get nailed too but that's nothing but a waste of time by the defense, which is exactly what we want. The tailback trails for the pitch that won't come then sets to protect the quarterback, who will already be searching for Beep. Stills plants and drops back after he fakes the pitch. He looks for the fly first, the buttonhook second, the sideline third, and if things have broken down around him completely the desperation shovel to the tailback fourth. It all happens fast and the defense initially has to read run for it to succeed. Unless we've been spied on this week that's what they'll do too. They'll bite and they'll pay for it. It seems like a gamble but it's really not. It's solid gold. The fly will be there. We haven't thrown a pass in the first period all season. The only gamble involved is my decision to try to pancake Grooms and that's strictly personal.

"Clean picture of you in the paper this morning, son," Stills says. "You psyched for what's-his-name's giant booty yet?"

"Getting there," I say. "How you feeling?"

"Feeling ready for some football," Stills says.

"Travis?" Mary Helen says.

"Play like you practiced Wednesday and we can mail it in," Stills says.

"I didn't think I did anything all that different," I say.

"You didn't," Stills says. "You just meant it more. My money says you'll be the third captain tonight."

"Order, Travis," Mary Helen says.

"Coming," I say.

Tyrone Davis begins to plead with his woman on the jukebox. He's a changed man. He's so lonely without her.

"That's sweet soul music, boppers," Stills says to the junior high trio. "Listen and learn."

I pay for my food and shake with the ten Mr. Shack gave me.

"Y'all take state for us tonight, Travis," Mary Helen says.

She counts back my change. The remark makes me grit my teeth but I look at the soft skin of Mary Helen's neck and the flash of anger melts.

"We'll sure try," I say.

I've said that or something like it a hundred times today without really thinking but this time I'm totally sincere.

Stills holds out a palm for me to slap as I leave.

"You the man, Codysan," he says.

The pickup doesn't have a radio in it so I drive and eat in silence, making do with a piece of "Hey Tonight" that's flying around in my head from when I woke up this morning. I'm holding my cheeseburger and shifting with one hand while I steer with the other. The shake is between my legs. The rings are in their greasy paper on the seat beside me. This is good food, especially the rings. *Louisiana Life* magazine did a story one time on choice side orders around the state and awarded five forks to these rings, which didn't surprise anybody in Oil Camp. The batter is crisp and spicy and the section of onion inside is sweet and crunchy. Most places will kill an onion dead. They'll do a tastectomy on it and it'll either be tough as rubber or limp as wet Kleenex. Not the Chowline. They serve you an onion that's still very much alive when you put your teeth through it.

Where I'm headed is way out in the country off the highway and down two dirt roads. Mrs. Hammontree stays out there by herself with a bunch of yard dogs. She has a son who lives the next place over and handles her cattle and she has neighbors not too far away but she won't let anybody except Mr. Shackleford or somebody who works for him touch her car, not even just to jump it off. It's an Edsel from 1958 and it's in as good a shape as a car that old can be. Mr. Shack and Big Daddy have been making sure of that since long before I went to work at the station. The car does need a new battery though. I've had to jump it twice already this month. I told Mrs. Hammontree last Saturday that she ought to let me bring a new one out and put it in for her but she said she'd tend to that when she takes the Edsel in for its next service interval. I think she just likes having somebody come out to her place.

I have mixed emotions about starting the car. Mrs.

Hammontree's not much of a driver anymore. She's not in near the condition her Edsel is. It swarms on her sometimes. It gets away from her. I've been seeing her around town in it all my life but lately it's pretty scary. To make a turn she'll come to a complete stop, cut the wheel as far as it will go to the right or left, then stomp the accelerator. No blinker or hand signal is involved. She doesn't drive as much as she aims. She finds a target and shoots her whole car at it. Other drivers absolutely do not concern her. She'll pull out in front of you and never know you're coming. The safest thing to do is keep an eye peeled and either park or go to the house when you see the Edsel on the loose. It's the only one in our parish and it's fire-engine red so there's no excuse for not giving it plenty of space.

I failed to do that one day last July and Mrs. Hammontree nearly got me beside the Piggly Wiggly. She was leaving the store and I was on my way back from Nita's. I had to run the Nighthawk up and over the curb. If I'd been traveling any faster than I was, I would have had to lay the bike down. I was just puttering along though, so I had time to react and dodge. I took the bump, stopped, and reviewed my blessings as I watched Mrs. Hammontree cross the railroad tracks up the street. She was unaware of what had almost just happened to a local youth.

Dogs come from every direction when I pull into the yard. There are at least a dozen of them in sight and no telling how many that aren't, hounds and spaniels and shepherds and others without clear identity. I hit my horn and drive over to where the Edsel is parked. Mrs. Hammontree comes out of her house wearing a plaid flannel shirt, baggy jeans, and black brogans. Her hair is silver and stringy and her face is tanned and seamed. I wait for her to calm the dogs before I open my door. She's carrying a switch in case one of them decides that he doesn't like the way I look. They're mostly friendly to me now that I've been out here a few times but there is one black-and-tan shepherd that will test me. His name is King. I don't see him.

"Morning, Mrs. Hammontree," I say.

"Hello, Travis," Mrs. Hammontree says. "Thank you so much for coming."

"You bet," I say. "When're you going to let me bring you a new battery out here?"

"Oh, I 'spect I'll have Mr. Shackleford or one of you boys install one of those for me next time I'm in for service," Mrs. Hammontree says.

It's unbelievable to me that she could think of Big Daddy as a boy. Me I can see, but Big Daddy? Not hardly. Mrs. Hammontree is definitely from the old school when it comes to race relations.

"Well, you could just about have bought you one with what it costs you to have us come out," I say.

"Never mind that," Mrs. Hammontree says.

I hook the cables up and start the truck. Mrs. Hammontree and her pack of dogs observe me like I'm the most interesting and entertaining thing they've seen all week.

"Where's King?" I say.

"King's somewhere," Mrs. Hammontree says.

No doubt. I sit in the Edsel and give it a try. The starter whines and the engine fights to turn over. When it does I don't think it's going to hold but I pump the accelerator and goose it on through. Mr. Shackleford told me before I came out here the first time that the Edsel was one of the biggest flops in the history of transportation. He said that it was introduced like it was the greatest human achievement since the flush commode but most people weren't impressed.

"Course it was a Ford so it was in a punting situation already," Mr. Shack said. "But it was ugly too and that's what did it in. The car just looked wrong. Thing appeared to have been designed by a blind man and put together by chimpanzees. The Ford higher-ups thought that if they slapped enough chrome on it nobody'd notice, but ugly is ugly and everybody did."

I actually kind of like the car. It is ugly but it's ugly in an interesting way. It's unique. It's from an era when you could tell what kind of a car you were looking at without having to read the name on the fender. These days they all look the same. They don't have any personality.

King trots around the side of the house while I'm undoing the cables. He paces and gives me the eye. I drop the hood of the Edsel and reach for the truck's. King moves in without barking. I greet him with a mouthful of sneaker and feel a sharp pain in my back. It doesn't last. Mrs. Hammontree lays her switch across the top of the dog's head.

"Shoo, King," she says.

King disobeys. He wants a piece of me. Mrs. Hammontree swats him again and he retreats sideways, growling. The hair on his back is up and his look is not diplomatic.

"He wouldn't really harm you, I don't believe," Mrs. Hammontree says. "He just acts a little testy around callers sometimes. Get, you."

King reveals his teeth for my benefit. I'm impressed.

"He's my third-oldest one," Mrs. Hammontree says. "I've had him for six years come January. My son purchased him from a fellow up in Arkansas. That's what he said he did anyway. I'm convinced that he won him in a card game but of course I've never actually said this to Clay."

She's rambling. Half listening I coil the cables and pitch them into the bed of the pickup. I keep an eye on King. He growls like he's trying to let me know that he'd take me out right here and now if it weren't for the old woman and her switch.

"He's always been bad to play cards for unusual stakes," Mrs. Hammontree says. "It's going to get him into deep trouble one of these days. Very deep trouble. It's a bad habit of his and I can't understand where he got it."

"Yes, ma'am," I say.

Mrs. Hammontree doesn't even pause.

"His father never wagered on a hand of cards in his life that I know of," she says. "I certainly never did. Clay was attracted to the wilder side from an early age though. He was always a taker of chances."

She's talking more to herself than to me now. I learned from Pawpaw that elderly people will sometimes do this. One thing will remind them of another and they'll forget where they are. Their eyes will get a distant, unfocused look in them and they'll just drift away. They'll forget that somebody's there listening to them and set sail into the past. You have to cut them off, which is rude and makes you feel like a jerk even though you know that it has to be done. You have to force them to return to the present tense.

"Mrs. Hammontree?" I say.

She's not quite ready. I shut the hood of the truck and move to my door. I let myself in. King barks like, "Next time, buddy. You and me."

"Take a break, dog," I say.

I roll my window down. Mrs. Hammontree is still talking.

"Ma'am?" I say.

I'm thinking: Earth to old lady. Earth to old lady. I try again, this time with a little more volume.

"Mrs. Hammontree," I say.

Her voice stops. She looks at me as if she has no idea who I am or what I'm doing on her land.

"Yes?" she says.

"Ma'am, I need to get on back to town now," I say.

Mrs. Hammontree's eyes begin to come back into focus.

"I'll wait and follow you in if you want me to," I say.

"Please forgive me," Mrs. Hammontree says. "There's no reason for you to wait. I wasn't planning to go anywhere until after a while."

"It's OK, Mrs. Hammontree," I say. "Just be sure not to turn your motor off for a little bit. That battery's pretty down but it ought to recharge itself enough to start you in twenty minutes or so. I'm sorry I can't stay longer.''

It's a double lie. I'm not sorry and I could stay if I wanted to. I'm not even sure if what I've said about the battery is true. It may be stone dead the second she turns the motor off.

"I understand," Mrs. Hammontree says. "No youngster I've ever known wants to sit around and listen to an old person on such a lovely day. I was no different."

"Yes, ma'am," I say. "Give us a call if your battery doesn't take."

I shove the stick up into reverse and back around to the edge of the yard. I feel guilty about not visiting a little more but I know that the longer I stay, the harder it will be for me to leave. Mrs. Hammontree is standing among her dogs like an elementary school teacher overseeing a class at recess. I wave to her before I go forward and she wags her switch in return.

Several of the dogs chase the truck down the first dirt road until they're satisfied that it's out of their territory. King is the last one to quit. He's probably the only one that was serious about it. I look at him in the rearview mirror. He's standing in the orange cloud I've made, baying victoriously.

10

I'm taking another way into town instead of using the highway. I turned off of it onto Thousand Pines Road, which goes out of Claiborne Parish and into Webster near Shongaloo where I'll pick up La. 2, loop around to the south, and come in on Old Store. It's a nice, Sunday drive–type route. Nita and I ride my bike out here all the time. Sometimes we go fast and sometimes we go slow. The cycle scares her a little so she holds on tight regardless of our speed. She presses her chest against my back and squeezes my hips with the insides of her thighs. The only way you can beat riding a motorcycle by yourself is riding one with a girl behind you. I wish that's what I was doing right now. As long as I'm wishing I might as well put us on a Sportster too, a jet black 883 with zero miles on the odometer. This would be its maiden voyage, Nita and me aboard with nowhere to go and all day to get there. Nothing would be bothering us either, nothing we hated from the past and nothing we feared from the future. We'd just be riding a motorcycle in a happy and endless present, connected only to each other, to the machine, and to the road. Time, along with all of our other worries, would have the afternoon off.

Seeing Mrs. Hammontree drift away like she did has put me in a strange mood. It reminded me of Pawpaw. He did that quite a bit even before he had his stroke. His mind was so tired and full of events that he couldn't keep everything straight. The details of his life had begun to confuse him. Sometimes he'd be in the middle of a story and either all of a sudden jump into another one that was totally unrelated or just stop talking altogether. That was bad enough but it wasn't as bad as when he'd call me Joe, which was my daddy's name. I always corrected him when he first started doing it.

"Travis, Pawpaw," I'd say. "This is Travis. Joe's boy."

"That's right," he'd say. "I know who you are, Travis."

Later I just let him go on with what he was saying because it got harder and harder for him to place me and I figured that what was happening to his memory insulted him enough as it was. He fought it hard but then the stroke hit him and there wasn't anything he or anybody else could do about it. He was going through his final lap, the one where he lost his way. The only good thing about his last six months was that he had his heart attack in the sixth and didn't make the seventh. His life was over before the attack but it could have gone on and on.

After he died I spent a lot of time listening to a tape of an interview I did with him for a junior high

English project. It helped me get over thinking of him ending up as a sick and pathetic old man who'd lost his bearings and made me start thinking of him when he was right, when his stories came one after another and his eyes shone with their telling.

Pawpaw taught me a lot of things. He taught me how to catch, clean, and fry fish. He taught me how to build a fire and read the woods. He taught me how to look people in the eye when I'm talking to them and how to shake their hands like I mean it. He taught me how to drive a standard shift, how to tie knots, and how to cuss. But most of those are things I would have learned anyway, things everybody knows. What I wouldn't have known without having been around Pawpaw for as long as I was is where I come from. I'm glad I have the tape as a reminder of that and of Pawpaw being Pawpaw and not some wasted shell in a hospital room.

The first sound on the tape is him clearing his throat. After that I say, "This is Travis Cody and I'm going to ask my granddaddy, Joe Glen Cody Senior, some questions about the old days. We're sitting in his kitchen on Gantt Street in Oil Camp, Louisiana."

"Are we on the air?" Pawpaw says.

"We're on the air," I say. "Let's start with when you were a boy, Pawpaw. You were born in Arkansas but you came to Louisiana before you started school."

"Tell you what, Travis," Pawpaw says. "If it's all the same to you I'd just as soon go back to before that. There's a few things I'd like to say for the permanent record. You've heard some of them before but you might not realize that they're important enough to re-member. This way they'll be remembered for you."

"You can go from wherever you want to, Pawpaw," I say.

"Good deal," Pawpaw says. "I'm just one little twig on a great big tree, same as you. Let's see here."

There's a short pause, then he takes off, outlining the general movement of the family from Georgia, where our greatest granddaddy landed after coming across the Atlantic from England as a guard on a prison ship, to Alabama, where Pawpaw's granddaddy's daddy fought in the Civil War, to Mississippi, where the Codys headed after General Lee's surrender, and finally to Arkansas, where Pawpaw's daddy was raised on a dirt farm near Junction City.

I went up there with Pawpaw a few times when I was real young and we walked around the erased home place. He pointed out what used to be and I tried to picture it. He spent his summers there when he was a boy and he talks about that on the tape for about five minutes. Then he gets going on the days when Sher-man's Store, which was what Oil Camp was originally called, became a boomtown and his daddy, my great granddaddy, brought his family to Louisiana because there was money to be made in the new field and all he had to look forward to if he stayed in Arkansas was a lifetime of trying to scratch a living out of ground that didn't want to give it.

"Daddy said, 'Thanks but I don't believe' to that piece of property when he heard they needed hands down here in the patch," Pawpaw says.

The Oil Camp stories are part Pawpaw's own and part ones he heard from his daddy, and I like them better than anything on the tape because they're closer to me. I know the places he mentions when he describes the busy oil and gas fields and the expanding, renamed town where more people lived in tents and shacks than in proper houses because they couldn't afford to be tied down if the drilling was to end all of a sudden.

"They came from all over," Pawpaw says. "They worked hard and they played just as hard if not harder. Lord, at the football they played around here back then. I've seen and been in some awful rough games in my time but nothing compares to what I saw as a kid during the boom because what they'd do is load the squad with drifters and outlaws and take on any eleven that was foolish enough to accept or extend an invitation. How they got away with it I don't know but it was a common practice in those days and places like Oil Camp took full advantage of it."

"This is football country," I say.

"Always has been," Pawpaw says. "Always will be. Rest assured of that. They played the other games tolerably well but just like now their heart wasn't in it. Baseball and basketball was a going-through-the-motions type of a deal. They was dead earnest about their football though. You probably don't know it but Centenary College of Shreveport used to field a team years ago. Had a hell of a run during the twenties and thirties, nationally recognized. The Gentlemen were giant killers back then. Things fell apart on them later but my point is that in the old days they'd occasionally have to pencil in a high school club or two to fill out their schedule. They put Oil Camp on the agenda once and only once. Agreed to come up here, did, and wished they hadn't because they got their collegiate behinds humiliated to a fare-thee-well that evening. Course they was playing against grown men. That wasn't no high school team they run into. Not by a mile. It was the saltiest hands from the patch and they just absolutely thrashed the pee-waddin' out of them poor Centenary kids. I couldn't have been more than eight or ten years old but I remember it plain as day. Seemed like they carted somebody off after near about every play."

"I can imagine what it must've been like when Oil Camp and Pineview played way back when," I say.

"Indescribable," Pawpaw says. "The neighbors took their football every bit as serious as Oil Camp did and they put uniforms on some of the orneriest customers in creation too. It was trash against trash and rough as a petrified cob. Them games wasn't games. They was brawls."

"Still are," I say.

"Still are is right. Nobody wants to beat each other as bad as Oil Camp and Pineview do. I guess you'll be finding that out for yourself before too long."

"I know about it already," I say.

"You just think you do," Pawpaw says. "You don't though. Not like you will after you been in one. Oil Camp and Pineview. There's nothing like it. I don't believe I ever saw your daddy get as upset and nervous as he did before his games with those green-and-white son of a bitches either. Course his bunch took care of them three straight times. I think that meant more to him and his friends than the two state games they won. Funny how everything always comes around to football, ain't it?"

"I wonder why that is," I say.

"I've always thought it was because football is the one game that most lets us be what we are, which is fighters," Pawpaw says. "I'm talking about folks who live a hard and dirty life, a rough life, and football is as hard and dirty and rough as it gets when it comes to the games you can play. It's hit and get hit, like a fight is, and the people who made this town, the men and the women both, loved a good fight. Somehow that got passed on. I guess it's just a blood-and-bone situation for those who happen to grow up here now."

"Must be," I say. "I know it's in mine. I love football."

"Something does seem right about it to a fellow," Pawpaw says. "Don't it?"

"Yeah," I say. "Something sure does."

"Makes you come alive," Pawpaw says. "Well now. You were asking about the boom, I believe."

"OK," I say. "How long did it last?"

"Big boom lasted nearly a decade before things started to taper down and a good many of the workers hauled out," Pawpaw says.

The Camp was thriving by then. It had a decent school system and there was plenty of work, both in the field and in the pine-rich woods, to support those who stayed. My great granddaddy stayed. He and my great-grandmother brought Pawpaw and his brothers up in the oil patch. They were a year apart, Pawpaw first, Max second, and Orval third. They all three began rough-necking as soon as they could and none of them finished their last year of school.

"That was a common mistake among the Codys," Pawpaw says. "I can't speak for my daddy or his or my brothers but that's one of the few things I'd do different if I had the chance. Your daddy was the first one of us to go all the way through high school. I was always proud of that."

Orval Cody was killed in World War II. Pawpaw and Max were in it too but they got out with only a shoulder wound, Max's, between them and came back to Louisiana when it was over. Max left after less than six months. He jumped a freight train and headed west. Pawpaw says that he thought hard about going with him but elected not to in the end because Oil Camp was his home and he wanted to keep it that way.

"I'd already saw what I wanted to of the world," Pawpaw says. "Unlike Max I knew there wasn't much in it that I wouldn't be able to find right here. But he was restless and bored and he'd never quite come to terms with Orval's death. I had steady work and I'd met me a gal that I fooled around and fell in love with. That was all I needed so I drove my stakes. Never regretted the choice either, except when your grandmother died on me but that was much later. I regretted everything when that happened, as a man will. I went through the same thing when your daddy was killed that afternoon, but that kind of regret don't last unless you let it. I done right. I was where I belonged."

He stops talking after he says that and neither one of us speaks for almost half a minute. Then I ask him another question.

"Looks like we've got enough room left for you to talk about your fight with Landreaux," I say. "Would you mind telling that to me again, Pawpaw?"

"Lord, I'd about forgot it," Pawpaw says. "You use to couldn't get enough of that one, could you?"

"It's a classic. Remember how you'd always start it off? You'd go, 'Well, sir, it was the greatest fight two twelve-year-old boys ever had in this town and you can bet your life savings on that.' Every time."

"Sounds to me like you ought to just go ahead and tell it yourself, Travis."

"You," I say.

"Well, sir, like you said it was the greatest fight two twelve-year-old boys ever had in this town and you can bet your life savings on that. We hit and kicked and bit and scratched and rolled on the ground and in no time at all I'd lost a front tooth and the other boy had an eye on him that was purple and swole up like a wasp done stung it. He was a coonass kid name of Pierre Landreaux whose family'd moved up here from the swamps and what our trouble undoubtedly boiled down to was we just needed to find out how much sand each other had. Turned out that both of us had quite a bit."

I knew that fight better than ones I'd been in my-self. I knew it like I'd actually seen it. They started at ten in the morning over by the cotton warehouses be-side the railroad tracks on Sherman Street and went at each other off and on for the next three hours. They covered over a mile, stopping every now and then to rest, and they wound up in the school yard, where they finally decided to call it a draw because both of them were spent and neither one could remember exactly what it was that set them off in the first place. Landreaux's eye was shut, Pawpaw's top and bottom lips were split, and they'd both scraped all the skin off their knuckles. It was probably no less than ninety-proof bull and that's why I had Pawpaw tell it to me so many times when I was a little kid. I wanted to see how he'd tell it again, what he'd add and what he'd take out. The basic elements were always the same though. The fight always started at ten, it always ended in a draw three hours later, and Pawpaw and Pierre Landreaux always went to the Foremost Dairy for ice-cream cones when it was over.

"We walked the whole way there with our arms on each other's shoulders," Pawpaw says. "We hugged each other like schoolgirls. He was my brand-new best friend and I was his. I told him, said, 'Pierre, from now on I'll do anything you ask me to but fight you,' and he said he felt the exact same way. We'd practically just killed one another and there we were, strolling along like the best two buddies that ever was. I believe I paid for the ice-cream cones. Old Landreaux. We played ball together. I wonder whatever become of him."

Hearing that story and all the others again on the tape restored Pawpaw for me. I'd like to say that I didn't pull away from him after the stroke but I did. I had to. I just couldn't take seeing him slip. I'd sit with him and wish I was somewhere else, anywhere else, because all he could do was lie there and stare at the ceiling. He was finished and it scared me so much that I put some distance between us to protect myself. I didn't even cry when he finally died. I did when I listened to that tape though. I broke completely down. It wasn't his fault that time whipped him. Time whips everybody. What I have on tape is the best part of Pawpaw's memory. He gave me that, trusting me with it in hopes that I'd hold it for him and put with it whatever it's going to be that I'll have to pass along when the time comes.

Pawpaw. He knew all these roads around here and most of the people. The church was packed for his funeral. It was standing room only because more than a man had passed. Brother Flournoy said that but I didn't understand what he meant until a day or two later when I dug out the tape and heard the familiar voice coming through loud and clear.

I'm turning left onto Old Store Road. The original settlement of cotton farmers was right along in here and so was the first strike. During the boom the town grew according to the lay of the railroad tracks and after a few years the bigger part of it was a couple of miles to the north. It was on the map and people quit calling it Sherman's Store almost immediately. They called it what it was. They called it Oil Camp.

And now it's dying. Somebody said the other day that there are currently only forty-nine working rigs in the state of Louisiana, the smallest number since they began keeping records. There aren't any at all in Claiborne Parish and that's a first in my lifetime. I can't remember ever not being able to drive around at night and see the lights of at least two or three.

Pawpaw drilled all over north Louisiana and south Arkansas. When he was still doing it and was on a site nearby he'd occasionally let me talk him into taking me with him to watch his crew on the job. Sometimes nothing much happens on a rig but other times it's like what being on a ship in a stormy sea must be. Guys are running all over the place and everywhere you step is wet and slick. Engines are roaring, iron is swinging, and everybody had better know exactly what he's doing because drilling for oil is fast and dangerous work. If you put your hands in the wrong place at the wrong time you'll lose some fingers or worse before you even realize that you've made a mistake. Pawpaw taught me some worm jobs like how to check mud and mix gel, but when they were making a connection or tripping pipe I mostly just stayed in one of the doghouses and watched the roughnecks. I liked the thought of being one of them when I grew up. I liked the word itself. *Roughnecks.* It sounded romantic to me, romantic but tough and mean at the same time. They put on their boots, their gloves, and their hard hats and they went out on the floor and got after her. They ran those stands into the hole. Watching them I'd think that it was just a matter of time before I'd be one of them myself. Roustabout, roughneck, derrick hand, driller. Just like Pawpaw. Just like Daddy. It was a clear and simple progression.

I changed my mind about it as I grew older and began to understand that there's no romance at all about being a roughneck or anything else in the oil field. It's nothing but a hard way to go. The saying is that to survive in the patch you need a strong back and a weak mind, which is generally true. At least if I do wind up out there it will only be a temporary situation, a means to an end.

Too bad college costs such a fortune. I took the ACT test in October and scored higher than I expected. It wasn't enough to get me a scholarship anywhere but I was slightly above the norm in everything, even math. I'm looking at my usual C in Alegbra II this six weeks. Algebra I didn't make much sense to me. Algebra II is incomprehensible. Lunk helps me out. He understands it. I don't know what I'd do if he didn't come over and make up problems for me before every test. He writes long strings of *X*s and *Y*s over square roots and other hieroglyphics then says, "Look, T, just do this."

Unlike Lunk, who wants to be an engineer, I'm way too daydreamy for mathematics. I'm not interested in questions that have definite answers. I like the kind that force you to ponder, come up with a thesis, and defend it. Mainly I like the first step, the one where you just ponder. Mr. Parke says that I'm a natural-born English major and that I ought to think about becoming a teacher. He knows about my goal of getting a college degree. He also knows that I'm clueless about what to study.

Life amazes me sometimes. It happens so fast. Blink once and you'll miss it. One day you're on a vacant lot pretending to be a football player and the next you're in a stadium doing it for real. One day you're a sophomore sub who can't wait to be a senior starter and the next you're getting ready for your last game. One day you're dreaming about your destiny and the next you're in it.

After I got hurt last season Mom said that time was going to start flying for me. She said I'd be out of school before I knew it but I didn't really believe her. Now I do. My senior year isn't even halfway over and it's already turning into a blur. The future is practically here.

I hit the horn when I pass Halliburton's house, which is just inside the Oil Camp city limits. Burt's A ROUGHNECK LIVES HERE sign is suspended from a facing board above the garage door. We've all got one. They're made out of plywood rectangles, black letters against a gold background. I guess I'll be taking mine down tomorrow and putting it with the scrapbook Mom's making for me.

I turn right at the Piggly Wiggly, cross the railroad tracks, and drag Main. The old hometown looks tired and wounded. It looks like the kind of place you'd want to get out of as soon as you could. I'll never leave Oil Camp though. No matter where I go I'll always be right here.

I check for the Lexus when I pass the Rexall. It's gone. Nita has shopped.

AFTERNOON

11

I don't have to clean the rest rooms today since I'm leaving early. Mr. Shack will take care of them before he goes this evening. Hallelujah to that. I'd rather do anything at the station than clean rest rooms. It's amazing how pitted out they can get in a day's time, especially the women's. The men's isn't exactly up to operating-room conditions, but one of the great secrets of the world is that females are three times bigger pigs than males when it comes to the use of public facilities. They'd just as soon drop stuff on the tile as take a shot at the wastebasket with it. My theory is that this is their revenge for all those centuries of picking up after everybody. It's a statement. They've decided that there's one place where they're by god drawing the line and letting somebody else pick up after them for a change. I don't really blame them but the result is that I never know what I'm going to encounter when I enter the Shackleford's Texaco women's room. There's always paper everywhere and dirty diapers sometimes lurk in the corners. I've even found discarded sanitary napkins on the floor in there. They've all been neatly wrapped in toilet tissue, but still. I mean come on.

No rest rooms for me today though. I'm done. I'm in the office peeling my coveralls off and getting ready to ease. The room smells vinegary like somebody has been dying Easter eggs. Mr. Shack obviously followed the directions in his Bunn-O-Matic manual while I was away. Now he's leaned back in his chair with his feet propped on his desk. He's working on a ham sandwich with leafy green lettuce hanging out of the bread. He's wearing his teeth for the occasion. He'll keep them in until he finishes his after-dinner wad of Levi Garrett, his dessert as he calls it.

"Get her commenced?" Mr. Shack says.

"She's running," I say.

"Too bad. That woman is bound to bump into something one day."

"As long as we keep on keeping that car going for her there's a chance."

"I think about it every time she leaves out of here. You off?"

"I guess so."

Mr. Shack takes a bite of his sandwich and chews for a moment.

"While before kickoff," he says.

"Six hours and twelve minutes. Not that I'm counting."

Mr. Shack swallows.

"You a liar," he says.

"I know it," I say.

Big Daddy opens the door and looks in.

"See you a minute, Travis?" he says.

"Be right there," I say.

Big Daddy closes the door. I hang my coveralls and cap on the stand. I take the rag off my head and toss it into the box beside the Coke machine.

"Come say 'bye," Mr. Shack says.

"I will," I say. "Reckon what he wants?"

Mr. Shack shrugs, chewing.

Big Daddy is standing in the wash bay with his arms folded. He looks like Mr. Clean.

"What's up?" I say.

"Been having my mind on you today, Travis," he says. "Been thinking about you and I wants to let you in on a secret. Come over here and take you a stance."

I walk across the gritty concrete and present myself to Big Daddy.

"Offense or defense?" I say.

"This for offense," Big Daddy says.

He hands me a can of Valvoline.

"Use this for the ball."

I arch my back to stretch it then settle into position. Big Daddy assumes a four-point stance in front of me.

"Look at my feets," he says. "Tell what you see."

"A pair of yachts," I say.

"Look again," Big Daddy says. "I'm giving you a sign."

I look closer this time and after a moment I notice that Big Daddy's right foot is a couple of inches out of line with his left one.

"What I'm fixing to do?" he says.

"You're coming right," I say. "To my left."

"How you tell?"

"Because you're cocked."

"Just the least littlest bit," Big Daddy says.

I stand. My back has a catch in it. I twist from side to side but I'm hurting.

"Why you showing me this?" I say.

" 'Cause," Big Daddy says.

He stands and puts his hands on his hips.

" 'Cause why?"

" 'Cause you needs to know it," Big Daddy says. "Grooms do this. He show you which way he going to come. I eye him hard the other night and he give his intentions away every single down. Right. Left. Straight ahead."

"Really?" I say.

Big Daddy holds up a hand.

"Gospel," he says. "Check him and see. He won't change. It's a flaw. Might be his only one but there it is."

"You should've coached, Big Daddy," I say.

"Just did," he says.

"Well thanks. What about defense? You got any defensive tips for me?"

Big Daddy lays his heavy hands on my shoulders. He bends over so that his face is directly in front of mine.

"One," he says.

"And?"

"Stay low."

He laughs his great laugh.

"Oh yeah?" I say.

"Yeah."

I fake a punch to his belly but he's so quick that he swats it aside before I can pull it.

"Been studying you all these years, Travis Cody," Big Daddy says. "Been studying you at work and been studying you on the ball field. I likes what I sees too. You a good boy. Don't know this Grooms but I bet he a pretty good boy hisself. Thing to remember is he a boy too. He big and swift and he know how to play but still he ain't nothing but a boy same as you is. Ain't nothing but a boy. You hear me?"

"I hear you," I say.

"Good."

Big Daddy holds his right hand out and I grip it the best I can. This is as close as I've ever felt to Big Daddy and it is a fine feeling.

Mr. Shack walks me to my bike. He has a chew the size of a golf ball packed into his left cheek.

"Well, Young Cody, I hear a man can have Oil Camp and points if he gets him a wild hair to wager," he says.

"How many?" I say.

"I been offered five."

"Take them," I say.

"Believe I just might," Mr. Shack says. "Course I'd feel a little better about the situation if I thought we had us somebody could handle the middle. I'm not convinced the one we got can do the job. You?"

He spits.

"All I know about the one we got is that he'll do what he can," I say. "He'll do his best."

"That'll be enough," Mr. Shack says.

"It'll have to."

The bell sounds.

"Knock his jockey strap off of him, Travis," Mr. Shack says.

He pats me on the shoulder before he moves away. I know how serious he is about tonight because he didn't call me Young Cody. He can't stay that way for long though. As I ride off I glance back and see him standing beside the customer's car performing his imitation of a punter missing the ball. Mr. Shackleford will be doing that to me when I'm thirty.

It's about an hour until we're supposed to meet at the stadium to pick up our jerseys for the pep rally. I need to start thinking Friday again. Rituals. What I'd normally be doing right now is sitting in fourth-period American history with an empty stomach because I didn't eat any of my dinner. I never can eat dinner on a game day. I always just pick at it, which is why I'm one of the few starters who does away with his whole pregame meal. I probably won't eat two bites this afternoon because of the Number Three cheeseburger, the rings, and the shake. They're settling well. I wish my back felt as good as my stomach does.

Foodwise I haven't followed my routine worth a flip today. I didn't eat breakfast and I did eat dinner. I'm not sure what I'll do with my pregame meal. I'm also not sure if altering my usual procedure will have any effect on what happens tonight. According to Mr. Parke it won't. According to Mr. Parke things turn out the way they turn out no matter what you do. I still feel uneasy about all these changes though. I guess I'll just have to get back on track at the pep rally. It'll be like Friday from then on regardless.

There's Nita.

She's crossing the highway on Main. I'll follow her and see how long it takes her to notice me. She may not see me at all unless I honk. Nita concentrates totally on whatever she's doing. Driving she looks straight ahead. She keeps her eyes on the road and her hands on the wheel. She's just the opposite of Mrs. Hammontree, whose eyes seem to be closed and whose hands seem to be in her lap when she drives.

I stay a couple of car lengths behind the Lexus. Nita lives over by the park. She goes west on Main, turns right onto Front, and takes another right onto Sherman. She's making the block. The cotton warehouses where Pawpaw's fight with Landreaux started are on my left. They've been divided into storage units of various sizes that hold just about everything you can name except cotton. Those days are long gone.

The light at the highway is green. Nita goes right again and we pass city hall. She hasn't seen me. The next light catches me. This is the one where my gears hung this morning when I was going the other way. I stop beside the Rexall. Across the street the bank thermometer is up to fifty. Quite a few people are out and about. I acknowledge waves and nods, lift a fist when I see Beep-Beep pass under the light. He's headed east on Main in his folks' Bronco. Lunk is with him. They spot me and Beep gets on his horn while Lunk crawls halfway out of the passenger-side window, raises his fists, and war-whoops. Beep stays on his horn until they're out of sight.

Waiting for the light I debate several options. I could chase Beep and Lunk and see what's up with them, I could run by the house and try to take a nap, I could go to the stadium and do another pool, or I could just stay behind Nita. I feel like I'm in a contest with myself to find out how many ways I can come up with to spend this hour. I better decide soon or it's going to be over and I'll have wasted it. OK. My back has begun to scream for attention so chasing Beep and Lunk and running by the house are out. It's either the stadium or Nita. Head or heart. My head says go to the stadium, do a pool, and then have Grease or Lyndon rewrap me. My heart says stay behind Nita because you never know. This might be the day. The light changes. I follow my heart.

Nita's just past the post office when I catch up with her. I thumb my horn. She'd never notice me otherwise. She looks in her mirror. She smiles. She waves over her shoulder, fluttering her fingers. I ease right up behind her. We pass the school. The sign out front is supported by a pair of miniature derricks, exact replicas of the big ones in the patch. It tells those who don't know that this is OIL CAMP HIGH SCHOOL. Under that is the reminder that Oil Camp High is the HOME OF THE ROUGHNECKS. The letters are gold on a black background. The bulletin board reverses that color scheme. Its current message is:

O.C. VS. PINEVIEW
STATE CHAMPIONSHIP
7:30 SATURDAY

We continue down the highway, which is officially called First East, through town, then we take a left onto South. The street runs beside the elementary school playground. It's one-way during the week. Some little kids are out on the dirt having a game of six against six. I honk at them. They show teeth, wave, and jump up and down. They're happy and free. Their football dreams are shiny and new. I don't envy them for what they're going to have to go through a few years from now but I do envy them for their dreams. I envy them for their make-believe game out there on that dirt.

Nita's house is two blocks ahead on Marietta Drive and when we get there I'm only slightly disappointed, the way you are when the fish you've just caught turns out to be too small to keep. You had the pleasure of bringing it in and you know that it'll be there next time and the times after that, but you have to hesitate for a moment before you put it back in the water because a fish is a fish. It bothers you to give one up. You forget about it almost as soon as it's gone though. You think: *Oh well.* You rationalize.

Dr. and Mrs. Tyler are home. At least Mrs. Tyler is. I can see her behind the kitchen window as I pull into the driveway behind Nita, who parks the Lexus beside Dr. Tyler's Grand Cherokee. I was hoping that nobody would be here. I was hoping that Nita and I would have the house to ourselves. This means that I may not get my back rubbed and that if I do there's no chance at all of it turning into anything else. The thought of reaching the final frontier was on my mind. It always is. I keep wondering when it will happen— not *if* but *when.*

It almost did last Saturday night. Mom was working late at the hospital. Nita and I were at the house. We'd been watching college ball on ESPN but we got to fooling around on the couch and by halftime I couldn't have told you who was even playing. I was thinking more in terms of buttons and zippers than blocks and tackles because it looked like we were seriously closing in on the point of no return. We were breathing hard and our hearts were thumping. I probably shouldn't have said anything but like a fool I did and it immediately broke the spell.

"What do you think?" I said.

"I think we better stop," Nita said.

"I don't," I said.

"I know," Nita said.

She moved away from me and began straightening her clothes.

"Why?" I said.

"Because I'm not ready for this yet," Nita said. "Don't be mad, Cody. I'm just not."

"What makes you think I'm mad?"

"The fact that you're a guy."

"Am not. I mean I am a guy but I'm not mad."

"Quit sulking then."

"Am I sulking?"

"You're getting ready to," Nita said.

"Sorry."

We didn't say anything for a moment. Nita got on her knees and took my face in her hands.

"What?" I said.

"I love you," Nita said.

"You do?"

"Cody."

"I could ask you to prove it," I said.

"Don't. It wouldn't be fair. Do you think I don't?"

"Don't what?" I said. "Love me or prove it?"

"Prove it. I think I prove it a lot."

"How?"

I could have named half a dozen ways but I wanted to hear her say some.

"By not going with anybody else," Nita said. "By walking to every class with you. By thinking about you all the time. Stuff like that. By letting you undo half my buttons."

"Do you think I love you?" I said.

"Yes," Nita said.

"Why?"

"Because I just do. You put up with me for one thing. Most guys wouldn't. Most guys are like, 'Put out or get out.' They're so immature about it. They're so pathetic."

"Answer me one thing," I said.

"All right," Nita said.

"Remember that day at the lake last summer?"

"Which one? There weren't but about fifty."

"The one when you told me you wouldn't mind being my valentine for life."

"I remember."

"That meant a lot to me."

"Me too."

"I'm holding you to it."

"I want you to."

"Will you make love with me sometime?" I said. "Technically I mean."

"Technically?" Nita said. She laughed.

"You know," I said. "Like really. Like not just this."

"Sometime I technically will," Nita said.

"Promise?"

"Cross my heart."

"Wouldn't it be weird if you finally decided to and I said I wasn't ready?"

Nita shook her head.

"It wouldn't?" I said.

"That's not what I meant," Nita said. "I meant that it'll never happen. You'll never not be ready."

"You're right about that," I said. "And I'll never quit trying to convince you to be too."

"You'll never believe this but I'm going to say it anyway," Nita said. "I don't want you to."

"You're over my head."

"I'm over my own head. This whole thing is. Just be patient with me."

"I'm trying," I said.

I drop my kickstand and take off my crash helmet. This would have been a bad day for such a major step anyway. It would have destroyed my concentration and I might have really hurt myself. Crews would have loved that. Oh well.

"I didn't think I was going to see you this afternoon," Nita says.

"Me neither," I say. "But my back is killing me. I hit a person and kicked a dog."

"Why did you do that? Who was the person?"

"Okie Colbert. I didn't punch him or anything. I just forearmed him. He was the one who's been making those calls I told you about. He did it again this morning."

"Figures. That Okie gives me the creeps. Every time I see him I feel like I need to go take a hot bath. What about the dog? You didn't hurt it, did you?"

"One of Mrs. Hammontree's. I had to go out to jump-start her car again. And no. You couldn't hurt that dog anyway. I was just keeping him from hurting me but I may have hurt myself. I don't know. Something did. It feels caught."

"Need treatment? Mom's here though. Daddy too maybe. He could give you something if it's really bad."

"He can't give me what I want," I say. "I want a back rub. From you."

"They won't care," Nita says. "I think Mom thinks we're farther along than we are anyway."

"You're kidding me."

"She's said some things."

"Like what?"

"Like just be careful mainly."

"Jesus God."

"Don't worry," Nita says. "Come on in."

"You got anything to carry?" I say. "This is embarrassing."

"Not anything you can see. I've been on a sleigh ride."

"A what?"

"Christmas shopping."

"Oh. I knew that."

I follow her inside wondering if my face looks as red as it feels.

The house smells steamy and good. Mrs. Tyler is cooking chicken spaghetti and baking garlic bread. She's wearing a pair of gray corduroys and an oversize white sweatshirt with a pin shaped like a sprig of holly on it.

"Getting ahead, Mrs. T?" I say.

"Occupying myself," Mrs. Tyler says. "I listened to those playoff games this morning and got all worked up. I thought I'd go ahead and cook because I'm going to be in such a state later on that I might burn the house down. This is for dinner tomorrow. You're invited."

"Great. I'll be here unless Grooms breaks my legs and I'm in the hospital."

"Don't you even think that, Travis Cody," Mrs. Tyler says. "If I ruin this we'll just order some take-out burgers and onion rings from the Chowline."

"Get a grip, Mom," Nita says. "It's only the state championship and it's only against Pineview."

"And I'm worried half to death," Mrs. Tyler says. "I don't see how you boys stand it, Travis. I've been thinking about y'all ever since I got up. Aren't you nervous?"

"Pretty nervous. But at least I won't have to sit and watch it. Once it starts we don't stay nervous for long. We just play."

"Well, I am one nervous cat about it," Mrs. Tyler says. "How's your back today?"

"That's why he's here," Nita says. "It hurts him and he wants it rubbed. Where's Daddy?"

"On the golf course," Mrs. Tyler says. "Where else on a Saturday? Here, Travis. Be honest now."

She holds a spoonful of spaghetti sauce up to my mouth. Her free hand is poised under the spoon in case of a drip. I draw some of the sauce into my mouth and taste it with loud smacks.

"Gross, Cody," Nita says.

I have eaten maybe five gallons of Mrs. Tyler's various sauces since I started coming around to see Nita. They're always stellar but this batch is not quite right. Something's missing. I can't place it.

"Is this a test?" I say.

"It is," Mrs. Tyler says.

"One more," I say.

"Let him feed himself this time, Mom," Nita says.

"I will not," Mrs. Tyler says.

"Don't get used to this, Cody," Nita says.

"You hush," Mrs. Tyler says.

She spoons me up another taste. I roll it around in my mouth. Mrs. Tyler watches me with an amused look on her face, which has only in the last couple of years needed any help from the makeup kit. Lines are beginning to form at the corners of her eyes and on either side of her mouth. Take them and the few gray hairs she has away and she could give Nita a run. They say that if you want a sneak preview of what a girl will look like when she gets older, the way her mother looks is a good one. Nita doesn't have anything to worry about if that's true. Mrs. Tyler is a beauty. She and Nita could pass for sisters in the right light. I wonder if she really believes we've reached the final frontier. I don't know why but it makes me feel self-conscious and dirty to think that she might. She likes me though. So does Dr. Tyler. I know that for sure. Mrs. Tyler told Mom one time that they're glad I'm Nita's boyfriend.

"She said they didn't care for the idea of Nita tying herself to one boy at first but you changed their mind," Mom said. "She said you were one of the most polite young men she's ever met."

"I've got her fooled then," I said.

"No, you don't," Mom said. "You are polite. Do you think Dr. Tyler would let you get within a mile of that house if he didn't like you?"

"I guess not," I said.

I used to believe that Dr. and Mrs. Tyler thought I wasn't good enough for Nita but that was more me than them. They've got money of the kind I'll never have and I let that bother me. Even now I can't help but wonder what they'd say if Nita and I ever really did get serious. It's easy for them to like me at this point. I'm only their daughter's boyfriend and their daughter will be going off to college next fall. She hasn't decided where yet, but it doesn't matter because wherever it is she'll be surrounded by rich guys from all over the place before she even gets her car unpacked. The possibility of losing her when that happens is in the back of my mind. I try to keep it there. I'm paranoid about that part of my future but it's something we'll be having to talk about soon and I dread it. One thing I know I'll tell her is that no matter what happens after we graduate I don't want her to think of me as an obligation. I don't want her to think it even if I end up in the same place she does. I'm not sure I believe it but I'm determined to say it anyway. Mr. Polite Nice Guy strikes again. I can't be any other way though.

I realize what's missing.

"Got any bell peppers handy, Mrs. T?" I say.

"You pass with an A-plus, Travis," Mrs. Tyler says.

"Come on, Cody," Nita says.

"Be gentle with him," Mrs. Tyler says.

"He's tough," Nita says.

The last thing I register clearly about the next twenty minutes or so is Nita saying that I smell like gasoline and me asking her what she expects me to smell like after half a day at a filling station. I'm lying on the carpeted floor of the Tylers' living room. Nita is beside me. I'm prone. She's cross-legged. My double-cotton is pushed up to my shoulder blades. The Ace bandage and the square of Pampers Grease cut for me are in her lap. The lights of the Tylers' Christmas tree are blinking on and off. I'm drifting in and out. Nita's humming. I don't recognize any particular tune. I close my eyes. I feel hands that are as good as ten whirlpools begin to knead the ache out of my back. I relax. I float. I doze. I dream about a beautiful girl running beside a lake. She's wearing a tight white bathing suit and she's running toward me. When she gets to me she puts her arms around me. She smells like Eternity.

12

I'm standing in front of my locker getting my game jersey on over the double-cotton. We're about to wear them to our second pep rally in twenty-four hours. It's not that we need any extra encouragement; it's just that Crews believes in routine as much if not more than I do. He and our principal, Mr. Acree, worked out the details for a rally today so that the last few hours before kickoff would be as much like a Friday as possible.

Some rapper is on the box putting forth badass verses. All around me guys are cutting up. They're whooping and hollering and dancing to the sledgelike beat. This is our last chance to act the fool because when we leave here we'll begin our gradual transition from thirty-two separate individuals with their own private hopes and fears into a single unit with a single purpose. It happens almost unconsciously, starting at the pep rally, continuing through the pregame meal, and culminating during lights-out. You're by yourself in the dark after Crews hits the switch, but you're making the final and most necessary connection with your teammates so you're not really alone. You can feel the energy building all around you. You send it out and you take it in and by the last few minutes of darkness the room seems to be roaring as if it contains a huge engine that has moved from idle to redline. Lights-out is when everybody begins to focus on the game and nothing else. Lights-out is when the whole starts becoming bigger and stronger than the sum of its parts.

I tuck in my double-cotton and jersey and button my jeans. I left the wrap off after Nita rubbed me down. I feel lighter and cleaner than I have all day. Somebody taps me on the shoulder. I turn around.

"Present for you, Cody," Lyndon says.

He hands me a brown medicine vial with a prescription sticker from the Rexall on it.

"What's this?" I say.

"Beats me," Lyndon says.

He adjusts his glasses and waits. I can tell that he's trying hard not to smile. I read the neatly typed prescription:

> Dr. Grooms
> 12/19
> Travis Cody
> Take two tablets when
> necessary for:
> MISSED BLOCKS,
> MISSED TACKLES,
> GETTING BEAT, and
> OTHER HEARTBREAKS

I twist the childproof cap off. Butterfly pills. I set the vial on top of my locker. Lyndon's backing away. He's nodding and pointing at me.

"Got you, Cody," he says.

I chase him into the training room, put him in a headlock, and administer noogies. Grease watches.

"You're a real clown, Lyndon," I say. "Moo like a cow for me."

Lyndon squirms. I've got him pinned against one of the padded tables. He might weigh 150 holding a couple of cinder blocks.

"I'm not letting you up until you moo like a cow for me," I say.

"Better moo, Lyndon," Grease says.

"Like a cow," I say.

Lyndon moos like a cow.

"Again," I say.

Lyndon moos like a cow again.

"One more time," I say.

Lyndon moos like a cow one more time. I release him.

"Good one, Lyndon," I say.

"Glad you think so, Cody," Lyndon says. "I couldn't resist. Want some fresh heat on your back?"

"I'll leave it bare for now. An angel from heaven just rubbed it for me. I'm feeling good. Real good as a matter of fact. Better than I have in a while."

"Lovely Nita," Grease says.

"What else did she rub?" Lyndon says.

He goes to the door.

"I think Cody got lucky today, y'all," he says.

Everybody who hears him over the cassette applauds. Beene sticks his head around the doorjamb. His hair is styled into cornrows. He pooches his lips out.

"Who?" Beene says.

Ransom joins Beene. He's also a sophomore but he doesn't start.

"It's bull, y'all," I say.

"Can't lie to me, Travis Cody," Beene says. "You been dipping on game day. Shame, shame, shame."

I shake my head. Beene holds a palm out. I slap it before I realize what's up. Beene grabs my wrist, draws my hand to his face, and sniffs. He has a better grip than I thought.

"It's funky," he says.

I jerk myself free.

"Get out of here, Beene," I say.

"Let me," Ransom says.

I offer him my hand and he inhales.

"Shoot," Ransom says. "Smell like gasoline to this nose."

"Yeah," Beene says. "From the Wild Thing pump. Yo, Cody. This Regular?"

I decide to play along.

"No way, bros," I say. "It's Premium."

Beene and Ransom like that a lot. Sophs. I slip past them. Hoots and whistles greet me when I step into the dressing room.

"Romeo, Romeo," Beep-Beep says. "Where you at, my happiness?"

"I hope you wrapped that rascal," Stills says.

It's major razz time but it doesn't last long because Lunk is getting everybody's attention by climbing onto the row of lockers in the middle of the room. He surveys the scene then points to the box.

"Turn that crap off," he says.

Lyndon shuts the rapmaster down in midrhyme. All eyes are on the Lunker. He has on the FOOTBALL IS LIFE T-shirt that he always wears under his jersey and he's scowling. He doesn't speak for a good thirty seconds. When he finally does it's a shouted question that we answer in unison.

"Who we gonna beat?"

"Pineview!"

"Who?"

"Pineview!"

"Who?"

"Pineview!"

Lunk runs in place and throws his arms in the air like a fighter who has just won his bout. Stills replaces the rap with something older and more affirmative, Sly & the Family Stone doing "I Want to Take You Higher." He turns the volume up louder than before. Jamming is renewed. Shirtless Beep joins Lunk on top of the lockers. Unlike Lunk's, which is shaped like a punchball, Beep's stomach is cut and honed. It's as well defined as the bottom of a turtle shell. Beep-Beep's a good dancer too, easily the best on our team. But Lunk's not bad. He's graceful for a big man. He and Beep are breaking all the way down. They're gyrating like a pair of berserk puppets up there.

I take the medicine vial off of my locker and shove it into my pocket. I move to the water fountain by the bulletin board. Van Noate's article and the pictures of Grooms, Lunk, and me are tacked to the cork. I drink some water then I look with respect at the thousands of tiny dots that create the image of Grooms. I wonder if I've been as much a part of his life today as he has of mine. I wonder if he has thought about me and checked out my picture. I wonder if he has any doubts at all about what he has to do tonight. I'd like to think so. I'd like to think he respects me enough to where I have at least crossed his mind.

Who we gonna beat?

13

I have to borrow Beep-Beep's comb at some point before we enter the gym. I'm real superstitious about this and even though we haven't ever talked about it I know that Beep is too because the exchange is always exactly the same.

Me: "Got a comb I can see a minute, Beep?"

Beep: "I reckon so, Cody."

I probably actually needed the comb the first time I asked him for it. When was that? I can't remember exactly but it had to have been sometime during our sophomore year because I can't picture a pep rally when I didn't do it. I even did it last year when I was out. Beep always has a comb. I don't know what I'd do if he didn't. I guess I'd have to ask him for something else, a toothpick or maybe a stick of gum. I'd tell myself that the object itself is secondary, that what matters is my question and Beep's response to it. That would be a lie though, because the comb is primary. I'll wring the little sucker's neck for him if he doesn't have one.

We're lined up according to class. The sophomores are first, then the juniors, then the seniors including Grease and Lyndon. Crews and Wroten are up front with the sophs. Crews will hold the door for us and he and Wroten will go in last. They'll sit on the bottom row with the seniors. The coaches have on black sweaters and ties. Grease and Lyndon have on black sweatshirts with O.C.H.S. FOOTBALL stenciled in gold arcs across their fronts. The rest of us have on our jerseys, home black with gold numbers. At chest level is the word ROUGHNECKS, also in gold. There's no other trim, only the numbers front and back—and the word.

Except for the section reserved for the team, the gym is absolutely packed. Cars and trucks were parked all the way over by the ag building two blocks from the school. I had to leave my bike on the sidewalk across the street because every cycle spot was taken. I don't guess I should be but I'm a little surprised that so many people have turned out for this. If you were a robber you could clean up in Oil Camp right now because nobody's home. You could fill a moving van. The town has come to a complete halt for the rally. One way of looking at this is to see it as a genuine show of community support. Another is to see it as nothing more than the ten-thousandth reminder of the huge death-or-glory deal people are making of tonight's game. I'd like to believe the first but I have a feeling that the second is probably closer to the truth.

I'm on the landing below the third-floor stairs behind Beep and in front of Halliburton, who is last in line. Everybody else seems fine but I'm getting antsy. I'm having trouble standing still. I listen to the crowd go through a series of yells in anticipation of our entrance. The noise swells and abates then it swells again. The space between each yell is punctuated by the scattery clapping of hands, the echoey pounding of drums, and the hissy shaking of aluminum cans with gravel in them. I glance at the sky through the tall rounded window at the head of the stairs. It's flawless, a hard and perfect blue.

"Y'all think Pineview's having one of these about right now too?" Halliburton says.

"I heard they was," Beep says.

I'm standing first on one leg then on the other. I must look like a little kid who needs to go to the bathroom. I've got to chill. I study the scuffed toes of my Chuck Taylors. I think of Grooms. I imagine him standing in his own school wearing his own jersey and getting ready to walk into his own gym for his own last pep rally. Does it mean anything special to him or is it just another day? Is it just business as usual for the studly Jericho? Surely not.

It's funny but I don't know Grooms at all except as a football player. He's a total stranger to me otherwise. I think I have a decent idea of what kind of person he is though. Big Daddy said that he's probably a pretty good boy and he probably is. You can learn quite a bit about somebody by playing against him. On the field Grooms is mean but he's clean. He never talks trash and he never holds. He just lines up, digs in, and hits you harder than you've ever been hit in your life. I've played a bunch of guys head-to-head and Grooms is the best in every way. A lot of them talk a much better game than they give you. They tell you what they're going to do to you and your family. They tell you what they're going to do to your mother and your girlfriend. They spit and they punch. They trip and they hold. Grooms is above all that. He doesn't play mind games. He just plays straight-ahead football. Bopping with a guy like him is a challenge but it's also a pleasure. Except for one play I actually enjoyed it the other night.

The memory of it comes back to me like a curse at the worst possible moment. I feel like I'm about to break out in a rash. I'm losing it. I've got to leave the line. I brush past Halliburton. He and Beep both say something but I don't answer them.

Pushing the sleeves of the double-cotton up, I skip down two flights of stairs to the first floor. The hall is in shadow because the lights are off. The sounds from the gym are distant, muffled. I can feel my heartbeat all the way up in my ears. I walk to the end of the hall and face a row of lockers. I take a three-point stance. I arrange my feet so that the toe soles of my All Stars are tight against the floor. I coil and strike. I forearm a locker, roll to my right, and come up ready-ready. I slam into another locker. Five times I do this. Hit, roll, ready-ready, hit, roll, ready-ready, hit, hit, hit. After the fifth time I rest my forehead on the cool metal of a locker door and bang the two that flank it simultaneously with the sides of my fists.

There were two minutes left when we scored from nine yards out on a quick-pitch to our tailback James Duhon going around right end. After a brief celebration of the touchdown, we looked to the sideline and saw Crews standing there like a statue. Crews is a big man. He's not as heavy as Big Daddy but he's almost as tall. He's always easy to find. He was holding the fingers of his left hand against his right palm above his head.

"Time, ref," Stills said. "I want a time."

The referee blew his whistle and waved his arms for a time-out.

"How many we got?" Stills said.

"One left," the ref said. "You're down to one."

Crews trotted onto the field and everybody in the stadium knew that we were going for two. Forget about overtime. We were going for the win.

Grease sprinted ahead of Crews with a basket of plastic squirt bottles. He had an extra one on his utility belt and it flapped like a holstered pistol. He set the basket down on the grass. There were four bottles in it. I didn't take one. I unsnapped my chin strap and tilted my hat back on my head. I was breathing hard. The guys who got the bottles from the basket drank from them then passed them on. Grease was taking care of the rest of us. When he came to me I opened my mouth and he squirted ice-cold Gatorade into it. I nodded and he stopped. I swallowed. My throat was so dry that I thought it would tear.

"More," I said.

Grease gave me another shot. I nodded again and he moved on. I swished the Gatorade around in my mouth, then spat it out. I pulled my headgear back into place and refastened my chin strap. Crews was on the hash mark at the twelve. He had a hand on Stills's shoulder. We formed a circle around them. Both bands were playing. We leaned in close. I was sure that Crews would call a pass but he didn't.

"Inside Belly Right," he said. "Now listen up. They'll be thinking pass or pitch so we're leaving the ball with the fullback. Jody?"

"Got it," Stills said.

"Do not pull the football," Crews said. "You hear me, Beene? You're carrying."

"Yessir," Beene said.

"Formation?" Stills said.

"Show them an I-left with your receiver split the other way," Crews said. "This is not an option, men. The fullback gets the football. Make him a crease, line. He needs three yards. Three yards."

His eyes were glittering.

"Time to run it, coach," the referee said.

"Let's go," Stills said.

"Get after somebody," Crews said.

I moved away from the group to the middle of the field and raised my arms.

"Huddle up!" I said.

I watched Crews and Grease jog back to the side-line. The team formed its huddle, which isn't really a huddle. We make two rows of five and Stills faces us with his back to the defense. Each of us has a designated place. I'm in the center of the row nearer Stills. We bend over with our hands on our knees and the other row stands. Stills puts his hands on my hat and calls the play. He's the only one who's allowed to speak after we've assembled.

"Here we go, y'all," Stills said. "Three yards and

we're out of here. We'll have their sorry ass. OK. This is I-left, Y open, Inside Belly Right on the first sound. First sound. Ready?''

He paused then we clapped our hands one time and together said, ''Break!''

Stills turned and I trotted past him. The nose of the football was positioned just behind the extra-point stripe three yards away from the goal line. Grooms was directly in front of it. He was resting on all fours. I crouched with my hands clasped, settled my feet, and reached for the ball. I fixed it so that when I fed it to Stills the laces would meet his right-hand fingers. Grooms rose into his stance. He worked his legs like a cat getting set to charge its prey. We looked each other in the eye. I bit down on my mouthpiece. Stills tugged the towel that covered my butt. He dried his hands and threw the towel onto my back. The bands had stopped playing but the noise of the crowd was like a wall. I felt Stills place his knuckles against my crotch. My eyes were locked up with Jericho's. I was listening only for Stills's count above the roar but I could also hear the voices of the Pineview guys as they hollered their defensive assignments.

''Strong left! Strong left!''

''Phantom go right! Phantom go right!''

''Roughnecks down!''

''Ninja take the pitchman! Ninja take the pitchman!''

''Covered!''

''Don't give the corners!''

''Readyset!''

"It's a pass! They're passing!"

"Coming at you, Phantom! He's coming across!"

"Dead meat! He's a dead man!"

"Hut!"

Grooms gambled on the count. He guessed and he was right. He would have been offsides if we'd gone on two, but we didn't and he moved precisely with the snap sound, ramming into me so hard and fast that he had me going backward before the ball even touched Stills's fingers. I knew immediately that it was all over. He was under me, the top of his hat planted in my front number. His momentum carried his head up my chest and slammed it into my chin. He was pushing me directly into the play and I wasn't strong enough to resist him. I was off balance. I was falling. I kicked a leg back for leverage and twisted. The muscles in my back strained against the pressure they were having to support. They stretched. They felt like they were being ripped apart and that's when I lost my will. Grooms pancaked me, met Beene at the four, and dropped him on the spot.

I was stunned. I was lying flat on my back and I wanted to stay there. Rolling to one side I watched Grooms get mobbed by his teammates. I listened to the jubilant noise from the Pineview stands. I closed my eyes. I was in so much pain that I didn't think I'd be able to get up but Lunk and Stills helped me.

"My fault," I said. "My fault, man. I wimped."

"You hurt?" Lunk said.

"I'm OK," I said. "Sorry, y'all. My bad."

Stills slapped the side of my hat.

"Shake it, babe," he said. "We got some time."

We didn't have enough though, and all I remember about the last part of the game is the shooting pain in my back and the sickening, nightmare feeling that I had allowed myself to quit, to surrender. I knew that Grooms would have beaten me anyway. He already had. But I hadn't fought him all the way down. Was it because I couldn't or because I just gave up? I guess I'll never know.

Pineview's final possession is a complete blank. I have no memory of it at all. According to the video I had a solo stop and an assist, both of which were meaningless. The Pelicans got the first down they needed to ice the victory and the clock was running. It was headed for zero. We called our last time-out but that only delayed the inevitable.

I feel heavy and sluggish, the way a panther in a cage must feel every time he wakes up and finds himself surrounded by steel bars that aren't going to let him escape. He may think it's only a dream sometimes but eventually he has to accept the fact that what has happened to him is no dream. It's real. It's his situation and it wears him out. All he can do is try to stay sane and hope that he gets a chance to do something about it.

I move slowly through the hall beneath the pictures of each senior class that line the upper walls of the old building. The rectangular frames are of uniform size and they're centered between the lockers and the high ceiling. The bottoms are attached but the tops are tilted out. The individual portraits are ovals. I find my parents' class and look at their faces. They were my age when these pictures of them were taken. Mom is smiling. Lisa Allen. Daddy isn't. Joe Cody Jr. He isn't smiling and he isn't looking straight at the camera. He's looking just enough to one side so that you can't make contact with his eyes no matter where you stand. I've never liked his senior portrait because of this. Mom says that she does. She says it reminds her of how sometimes when they talked about something really serious such as being in love with each other he would focus on the side of her face like he was too shy to look her in the eye. She says that this was an endearing quality and always adds, "One of his many." When she says it she looks happy and sad at the same time and I know that she has never gotten over losing him. Maybe you can't get over something like that. Glen and I lost him too but that's different. It must be the most awful thing in the world to have the person you love and think will be with you forever taken away from you the way Daddy was taken away from Mom. They were just getting started. They had no idea.

For a long time after the accident I kept having this dream where I asked Daddy to stay at the house with me that afternoon and he'd do it. We'd get the football out and throw it back and forth in the side yard. I'd catch it and run toward him. Usually he'd let me past him but sometimes he'd grab me in his arms and take me down. I could feel his strength as he held me against his chest for a second before gently putting me onto the grass. When I woke up I could still feel him but I knew even before I opened my eyes that he was gone. It was just a dream. Eventually I quit having it.

I make sure that once in a while I hug Mom and tell her that I love her and appreciate what she's done for me. I probably don't do it enough. She gave herself to Glen and me after Daddy got killed. We were her top priority and I think that's the main reason she stayed single. She's had several boyfriends, of course, including two or three that I've seen at the breakfast table. She never got too serious about any of them though, and that's her business. She has her reasons. Pawpaw helped her some moneywise but for the most part Mom has made her own way. She sure didn't get anything from her folks. They split up a couple of years after she and Daddy got married and they went their separate ways. They started new lives that didn't include their daughter. I've never met them and Mom doesn't mention them. It's like they don't exist.

None of that happens in these pictures though. In these pictures of them Joe Cody Jr. will never have to die and Lisa Allen will never have to raise two boys alone. They'll never have to know. They'll just be seventeen years old eternally, a good-looking senior couple with a long and happy future ahead of them.

God, life's weird.

I take a deep breath through my mouth and hold it for a moment before releasing it slowly through my nose. I feel myself begin to calm down so I do it again. It's like a church in the hall, hushed and peaceful. I wouldn't mind just blowing off the pep rally and staying right here for the rest of the afternoon but I can't.

I've got an obligation. I head for the stairs. As I climb the first flight I realize that I've knocked the scab off an old cut on my right forearm. The cut has been with me since Bataan back in August. I used to notice it. Now I don't, the same way I don't notice the stiffness in the elbow I tore up last year. It's just there being a part of me.

"You all right, man?" Halliburton says.

"Had to take a leak," I say.

"Well, you done sprung one," Beep says.

The blood from the cut is running down my arm and palm and dripping off my middle finger. I make a crude heart on the floor with the drops then wipe blood on my jeans. I bend over and hold the cut against my thigh to stop the flow.

"I'll live," I say.

"Listen," Halliburton says.

"Crazy cans," Beep says.

Oil Camp fans traditionally carry aluminum cans that are half-filled with pea gravel to pep rallies and games. Van Noate wrote an article about it one time. He said that the sound of those cans and Oil Camp football are as linked as cheerleaders and pompons, marching bands and halftime, popcorn and movies, and fireworks and the Fourth of July. When the hiss of the gravel reaches a peak, the crowd starts a chant: *"Let's take state! Let's take state!"* We join in, each of us jabbing the air with an index finger. Crews opens the door and stands against it. The line moves forward and even before all the sophomores are inside, the crowd abandons the chant and replaces it with a noise you feel like you could reach out and touch. It's a roar so intense that it sounds almost desperate. It gives me goose bumps.

"Got a comb I can see a minute, Beep?" I say.

"I reckon so, Cody," Beep says.

He takes his comb from the back pocket of his fatigue pants and gives it to me. I'm aware that we won't ever do this again. Time is in motion and there's no way to stop it, no way to slow it down. This is a day of final things. My life, all of our lives, will be different tomorrow. I run the comb through my hair. When I return it to Beep I notice that my hand is shaking.

I pass Crews and Wroten. Crews nods. His face is serious but not as serious as Wroten's. Nobody can make a face as serious as the one Wroten wears on game day. His teeth are clamped and his jaw muscles are jumping. He's grave almost to the point of being comical. He doesn't nod. He just looks right through me.

The band is directly across from us. They strike up the Oil Camp fight song as we take our places, which are marked by Powerhouse bars with notes taped to them. The pep squad is responsible for the candy and the notes. I pick mine up but I search the stands for my people before I read the note. Nita's the easiest to find because she's on the front row of the band. She plays flute and she's also a majorette. She's looking at me. I grin at her and she grins back, then she cuts her eyes toward Billy Fanning, the drum major. Billy's directing the fight song, which has no words. It's the Olympic Games theme from television played in double time.

Mom is the next one I see and Glen is with her. They're in the section behind the band. Mom has a hand over her mouth. I wave to her and she takes the hand away from her mouth to wave back. Her lower lip is caught between her teeth. It must be something for her to see this. Not long ago she was standing where Nita is and Daddy was where I am. She's seen it before with Glen and me both, but I would imagine that it always brings back the kind of memories that aren't easy for her to handle. I show Glen a fist and he raises one in return. He still has on his work clothes so he must have just rolled in from delivering that 'dozer to Winnfield. I didn't expect to see him here.

Mr. Shackleford and Big Daddy are standing with a group of men against the far wall underneath a DO IT TO IT ROUGHNECKS banner. When I catch Mr. Shack's eye he immediately goes into his punting pantomime, which gets a thumbs-down and a smile from me. Big Daddy just shakes his shiny head.

I don't see Mr. Parke or the Tylers. I know that Mr. Parke is here though, because I saw his car parked on the street by the sidewalk where I left my bike. He must be on this side of the gym. The Tylers probably are too if they came and I'm sure that at least Mrs. T did.

I check my note. It's typed and it's identical to everybody else's. There are thirty-six of them, one for each of the players and ones for Grease, Lyndon, Crews, and Wroten. Today they say, "Good luck tonight! Go Roughnecks! Punish the Pels!" Yesterday they said, "We love you! Go Roughnecks! Take state!" The pep squad poets keep their messages short and to the point.

This is a bigger deal pep rally than I've ever been a part of because the whole town is here. I'd bet money that there aren't two dozen people who could have made it but didn't. It's incredible. There's enough energy in this gym for a week's worth of statewide electricity and I feel guilty about doubting these people's appreciation and support. The vibes in here are totally positive, at least on the surface. There's something strange about it but it's quite a scene.

The rally follows the usual pattern. Everything about it seems somehow magnified though, transformed. It's like we're braves and the tribe has gathered for one last ceremony to reassure us, to bond with us, and to offer us inspiration before we go to war. The cheerleaders lead half a dozen or so call-and-response yells; the band plays a couple of numbers; the majorettes do their "La Bamba" routine, inspiring Beep-Beep and Halliburton to poke my ribs with elbows I barely feel because I'm concentrating on the beauty and grace of Nita's movements; then Tiffany Ward, the head cheerleader, asks Crews to come out and say a few words. He receives a standing ovation on his way to the mike, which is set up at the free-throw line to our left. He adjusts it to his height, taps it twice, and opens his mouth to speak. But the applause doesn't stop, so he steps back and waits. He holds up his hands when he's had enough.

"This football...," he says.

We quit clapping and sit back down.

"This football team has had twelve sweet highs and one bitter low this season," Crews says. "I won't say that they'd trade the twelve to change the one, but I will say without reservation that there are thirty-two young men over there who feel extremely fortunate to have the opportunity of doing something about what happened to them down in Pineview a few weeks ago.''

He lets the outburst of howling and applause run its course.

''We have eleven seniors on our football team this year,'' Crews says. ''Nine of them are players, one is our manager, and one is our trainer. Those nine senior players have been with our program since they were in the seventh grade. They've seen classmates of theirs come and go along the way but they stayed. They may have wanted to quit at times but there was something deep down inside of them that wouldn't let them do it. Some have never made the starting lineup. Others have started every game for us from junior high on up. All of them have contributed. They've given everything they had in games and on the practice field because that's what has been demanded of them. Nothing less is acceptable. They came to us knowing that and they've clawed and scratched and done whatever it took to be a Roughneck. This game tonight is theirs. It belongs to them. They made it happen and I'd like for them to step out here and tell you what it means to them. Seniors? Grease, you and Lyndon come too.''

Jesus. Lunk and Stills are used to this. They're our permanent cocaptains and they address every rally. I've never had to talk in front of this many people in my life. My heart is in my mouth. I walk out feeling weightless. I take a spot at the end of the line. Grease and Lyndon push me over beside the other players.

"You need a Band-Aid, Cody," Lyndon says. "Here. Go wash that off before you put this on."

I can barely hear him because of the noise in my head. Part of it is from the band and the crowd but most of it is from the blood that's rushing through my body. I cram the Band-Aid in my pocket without looking at it. Stills is going first. I don't listen to him. I don't listen to anybody. I'm trying to think of something relatively unstupid to say myself. My heart is slamming. My throat is dry. My brain is empty. I want to run away. I'd rather eat glass than face this many people.

"Go ahead on, Cody," Grease says.

It's my turn. I walk to the microphone. My legs may buckle under me at any second. Everybody's looking at me and it's so quiet that I can hear the crinkling of my candy bar wrapper as I worry with it. I'm crushing my Powerhouse.

"Uh," I say.

I'm too close to the mike. It feeds back and I flinch, which causes a good deal of laughter. I pick out a sneaker skid on the gleaming wooden floor about five yards in front of me and stare at it. I flash on the idea of going on a tirade about how hard playing ball in a town like Oil Camp has been for me. I could talk about how at times I've hated the coaches, hated the expectations, hated the people who watch and judge us. All of that is true but it seems distant to me right now. It seems out of place. Saying it wouldn't serve any purpose.

"Any year, if you don't mind, T," Lunk says.

Suddenly I know exactly what I'm going to do. I'm going to tell them what they want to hear, just like I did back at the Chowline when that kid asked me if we were ready to kick Pineview's butt. This is just as true as all that other stuff. I draw a breath and go.

"We're twelve and one," I say. "And you're looking at the reason we're not thirteen and zero."

My voice sounds odd to me at first but my brain is functioning again so I continue.

"I missed a block the other night and it cost us a football game," I say. "It cost us the district title. I haven't slept real well since then even though some of y'all have told me that one man can't lose a game by himself. I've appreciated that. I really have. Sometimes I even think I believe it. Then I remember that missed block and realize that because things fell the way they did I have to take the blame. I got beat and we lost because of it. It was my fault. Nobody will ever totally convince me that it wasn't and I want y'all to know that I'm sorry for letting it happen."

I shuffle my feet. My Powerhouse is mush. I'm still staring at that mark on the floor but I'm not nervous anymore.

"You'll get him tonight, Cody," somebody says.

I nod. I look up for the first time. I glance around the gym and for a moment I waver because all I can see is a group of people who are living out their failed lives through me, through us. But that's an unfair vision and it passes before I let it derail my train of thought.

"Like I said," I say. "I'm sorry. But there's not much I can do about that now. And regardless of what you think, whether it's that we lost that game strictly because of me or that no individual player ever gets his team beat by himself, that one is over and done with. It's history. It's old news and I'm getting real tired of worrying about it. I'm getting real tired of worrying about that game and living with that play. All of us are. We're sick to death of it. A while ago Coach Crews said he wanted us to tell y'all what this game means to us. Well, it means a lot. Maybe we've let it mean more than it should. I know I have. I've tried not to but there's no way around it. I have to admit that I sometimes wish it didn't, but I'm looking around and realizing how much football matters to this town. So here's the deal. This game tonight means three things to me. First, it means that I'm fixing to finally be able to quit worrying about that other game. Second, it means that I'm fixing to quit having to live with that play. Third, it means that I'm fixing to get the best night of sleep I've had in a month. It means these things because me and these guys are going to be state champs when it's over. Believe it, Oil Camp. Come about ten o'clock this evening the title will be back where it belongs."

I say, "Thank you," but it gets blown away by the first standing ovation I've ever been given. The band is playing, the crowd is going nuts, and I'm overwhelmed to have this much emotion directed at me. I'm standing here with wet eyes and something that seems as big as a tennis ball stuck in my throat. I feel liberated.

Grease's speech is only three words long. Lyndon's is two words shorter than that.

"What Cody said," Grease says.

"Yeah," Lyndon says.

As always the rally concludes with the Oil Camp High alma mater. The rest of the team joins the seniors out on the floor. I wedge myself between Lunk and Stills and we put our arms around each other's waists. We face the wall where the words to the alma mater are posted on a huge black-and-gold sign that's surrounded by all the O.C.H.S. championship banners. We sway back and forth as we sing. I squeeze Lunk and Stills tight when we get to the last line of the song and they squeeze me back: *Oil Camp High School hail!*

The cheering that follows is loud and prolonged. I remove my arms from Lunk and Stills and raise my hands for fives.

"I love you bastards, man," I say.

It just comes out. I half expect a smart remark from one of them but it doesn't happen. We're riding too high. Our emotional fences are on the ground. We're friends. We're homes. There's no sense in trying to deny that love is a part of it.

Afterward Mom and Nita hug my neck and Glen and Mr. Parke shake my hand.

"I'm so proud of you, Travis," Mom says.

"I didn't know if you'd ever say anything but you were pretty great once you did, Cody," Nita says. "Pretty dang great."

"Couldn't've said it better myself, little bro," Glen says.

"Very nice," Mr. Parke says. "Very nice indeed."

I was wondering if I did the right thing. Evidently I did. I feel kind of naked though, kind of raw. I just told my worst secret in public, part of it anyway, and everybody thinks I'm a class guy. Maybe that's what I really want.

"Thanks, y'all," I say. "I guess I talked the talk."

"You talked it all right," Glen says. "Now all you have to do is go out there and walk the walk."

"That's all," I say.

14

You know as soon as certain things happen to you that they're important enough to be permanent. Some you wad up, cram as far back in the closet as you can, and try to ignore. Others you fold, place gently in the top drawer, and cherish. That's where my standing ovation is headed. I'm still grinning about it. Tonight's game may not make the cover of *Time* magazine next week but it does matter to a lot of decent people. The standing O showed me that. It also allowed me to believe that more of those people than not really are behind me, behind us. I haven't been able to do this lately without some kind of negative qualification. I like this better. Being pissed off at folks isn't my style.

I don't recall ever feeling this calm after a rally. Normally I'm juiced to the tenth power. I'm ready to pad up and play right then. Not today. Today I'm tranquil. It won't last but I'm relaxed and serene for the time being. I probably could go to sleep but I'm not going to let myself do that because I might ruin this glow with the wrong kind of dream.

I slide away from everybody so I can clean my arm off in one of the rest rooms. The cut's not bleeding anymore but I go ahead and attach the Band-Aid Lyndon handed me a while ago. It's decked with tiny drawings of Superman, which is typical Lyndon foolishness. He can't just give you a regular Band-Aid. He has to give you one that has a cartoon hero on it. Superman does seem appropriate though. Maybe some of his strength and speed will rub off on me.

I walk down to the cafeteria, hoping that nobody shows up wanting to hang out. I can hear the cooks banging around in the kitchen. They're getting our pregame meal together. It's a simple menu designed to go easy on the stomach. Dry roast beef. Dry toast. Half a canned pear on a leaf of lettuce. Ice tea. I usually down it all, even the lettuce. But I'm not hungry this afternoon so I probably won't eat a bite, which if I don't will be just one more deviation from my normal pattern. I've been thinking ever since I got up this morning that I'd be well into my routine by the time the pep rally started, but about the only things I've done according to my customary rules of superstitious game-day behavior this time are wear the double-cotton and borrow Beep's comb. Mr. Parke would be pleased. He'd say that I'm headed in the right direction. I wouldn't start a major argument with him about it but I could have picked a better time than the day of the state championship game to throw my nets away.

"I've never worked without them," I'd say.

"Don't you think you've always worked without them?" Mr. Parke would say.

"No," I'd say.

But I'd wonder. Mr. Parke knows how to make you wonder. He's not even here and he's making me wonder.

I take a seat at a table near the back of the cafeteria, one of the ones covered by shadows. Dusty rays of bright afternoon sunlight are slanting through the windows on my right but they don't reach this far. I lift the front of my jersey with my thumbs and forefingers. ROUGHNECKS is upside down and backward. It looks like Russian. After tonight this jersey and my gold road one will be mine to keep. Crews gives them to the seniors each year. The sophomores and juniors have to check theirs in. I'll probably let Nita have mine. She already has my sophomore jacket, my only jacket. I don't know if she'll want this year's or not. I don't know if I'll want it or not. It depends on the second patch and the second patch depends on what we do tonight. The first patch is a done deal. It'll be shaped like a football and say DISTRICT 1AA RUNNER-UP. The second patch will either negate that or verify it. It'll be shaped like Louisiana and say CLASS AA STATE CHAMPION if we win, CLASS AA STATE RUNNER-UP if we lose. I can't speak for Nita but I don't think I would want to wear a jacket with two runner-up patches on it.

I put my feet on the table, cross my ankles, and think about what Crews said at the pep rally: They've clawed and scratched and done whatever it took to be a Roughneck.

My feelings about Crews are complicated. I've loved him and I've hated him. I've resented him and I've appreciated him. I've cussed him and I've thanked him. He made me what little bit of a football player I am during Spring Ball following my ruined junior season. He rode me extra hard for twenty consecutive days. He tested me for four weeks. No matter what I did it wasn't exactly right. If I blocked somebody five yards back he wanted six. If I tackled somebody at the line he wanted a loss. I was in better shape than I've ever been in but he almost broke me. He pushed me past where I'd been able to push myself and I thought I'd pushed myself as far as I could go.

"You want to be a Roughneck, Cody?"

Crews must have asked me that a thousand times during those twenty practices and I always gave him the same answer.

"Yessir."

I said it even when I wasn't sure I believed it.

I went down against Plain Dealing. It was the fourth game of the season and it was over early. We were up 41–0 at the half. During the break Crews told the first offense and defense that he was going to give us one more series both ways, then he was going to let us call it a night so the subs and scrubs could get themselves some licks. Several of them had already played but now they were going to take over and work as a unit. I celebrated by eating a Hershey's bar with almonds and chugging a couple of Cokes. Except for punts, if we had any, I was as good as done for the evening. I was feeling pretty loose.

We kicked off to open the second half and held. The Lions were baked. They didn't have much to start with and after the pounding we'd given them, they didn't have anything left at all. The guy they had at center and nose was breathing like a wounded animal. He was short and baggy and in no kind of shape for what he was being asked to do. I'd pushed him around like a checker all night and I really teed off on him on first down after their punt.

"God dang, man," he said as I helped him up. "Don't y'all have a second team?"

"They'll be out here in a little bit," I said. "Just come on and play some ball with me."

"I'm trying to," he said.

I almost felt sorry for him.

We huddled up looking at second-and-two. Stills called a handoff to the tailback headed left. We broke. We trotted to the line of scrimmage pumped and confident. I was wondering if I'd get to punt before the game was over. I hoped so because I wanted to pick up my junior letter that night. It takes sixteen quarters to letter and one play in a period counts as a quarter. I was daydreaming about being a three-year man like Daddy and Glen, but I knew I'd have to wait a week unless the subs got into a punting situation in the fourth quarter.

Stills set us and the Lions braced. I hiked the ball on the second sound and charged but the noseman ducked his shoulder. He eluded me like we were playing tag. It wasn't a stunt. He just dodged me and nobody filled the gap. I entered the empty space and put my left hand down to catch myself. The next thing I knew I was puking and seeing paisley patterns. Lunk reconstructed the play for me later. Halliburton at left tackle had driven his man back, to the right, and over to where my momentum had carried me. Together they weighed close to five hundred pounds. My arm had locked when I put my hand down and it gave under their weight. It collapsed like a folding ruler the wrong way. It snapped. I've never looked at the video. I took Lunk's word for it.

"Don't," he said.

One of the officials was on his knees beside me. Lunk, Beep-Beep, and Halliburton were standing behind him. The official was telling me to hang on. I asked him if we got the first. I was lying there with my arm turned inside out, I had just chucked lunch in front of a stadium full of people, and all I could think of was the first.

"Don't worry about it," he said.

He probably thought I was raving and I guess I was. But for some reason the first down seemed like the most important thing in the world to me at that moment. I looked up at Lunk. He showed me four fingers. We'd made it by two yards. I blacked out.

A Shreveport surgeon named Davis Wilcox put my elbow back together the next morning at Schumpert Memorial Medical Center. That afternoon he told me that it would be as good as new once it mended.

"Even better," he said. "You've got yourself a bionic elbow there, Travis."

"How long?" I said.

"A while."

"Am I out?"

"I'm afraid you are."

Lunk, Stills, Beep-Beep, Halliburton, and Grease came over to see me on Sunday. We watched the Saints lose to the Falcons on TV. At first I was glad that all my buds had come, but I felt horrible and wasn't into them being there after about half an hour because all they wanted to talk about was Oil Camp football. I was disconnected from that and from them. The Saints didn't help the situation either. The offense couldn't move the ball and the defense finally got worn down and gave up two late touchdowns for a 27–10 final. It was a long, depressing afternoon.

Dr. Wilcox released me from Schumpert on Monday and Mom drove me home. It was raining hard when we left Shreveport and as we crossed the Red River bridge we got into an argument about when I should go to the stadium. Mom said that I shouldn't until I'd returned to school. I said that I was returning to school the next day and that I was going straight to the stadium as soon as we got to Oil Camp.

"You can either drop me off or I'll walk," I said. "I need to talk to Crews today."

"He knows your predicament," Mom said.

"You don't understand, Mom. I need to go over there today. I have to find something out."

"You can't do anything with that arm like it is if that's what you're thinking. Dr. Wilcox said you're out."

"I might can do something. I'm not that out. I'm still on the team."

"You can't play football."

"Don't say that. Please don't. Maybe I can punt."

"How will you catch the ball?"

I closed my eyes. I couldn't believe what had happened to me.

"I need to go," I said.

"Why?" she said.

"I just do."

"Fine. You just go right ahead on then."

"I will."

The argument was over. I'd won and we weren't talking anymore. We drove in silence. The only sounds in the car came from the motor and the windshield wipers. The motor hummed and the wipers slished back and forth on the wet glass. I opened my eyes and stared out the window. We didn't say a word. I burrowed into our silence.

The whole time I was in the hospital I'd hoped that somehow my injury wouldn't transfer into the real world intact. I knew that it wasn't going to go away entirely but I honestly thought that it might be less severe on the outside. Now I was getting my first dose of the truth. The injury was just as bad. It hurt just as much. A new week was under way and it was leaving me behind same as the next eight to ten of them would depending on how I healed. It was like opening your front door and discovering that you've been robbed. I was really out, really shelved, really on hold. In the time it took me to get fallen on I was through for the season. I'd tried to come to terms with that fact but I couldn't. I wasn't ready to accept it yet. The idea that I'd be able to talk Crews into letting me into a game for one play was in the back of my mind. I was that close to my junior letter and I thought that if I could get it, being out would be easier to tolerate. All I needed was one play.

Pine trees and red-clay ditches flanked the highway between Minden and Pineview. I imagined that a stout blade extended from the front bumper of the car and mowed down the trees on my side as we passed. I imagined that I was lashed to their trunks. I wanted to tear my hair out. I wanted to scream. One play. What a fluke.

Mom cracked her window and lit a cigarette as we were circling the square in Pineview. The town is laid out so that you have to do a three-quarter turn around the courthouse if you're headed north on the highway. Southbound traffic goes straight through but the northbound lane takes you on the scenic route because whoever planned it wanted to make sure that all travelers passing through going north notice that Pineview is the seat of our parish. The courthouse is on your left. The stores are on your right. The joke in Oil Camp is that you'd have to do the square twice before getting on with your trip if somebody in Pineview could figure out how to draw the letters for a sign.

I moved my imaginary blade to the other side of the car and used it on the statue of the Confederate soldier, the magnolia trees, and the courthouse columns. I knew that Mom was about ready to say something. I waited while she worked on her cigarette and made up her mind what it was going to be.

"Does it hurt?" she said.

"Not much," I said.

"Tell me if it does."

"I'm fine, Mom. I'm OK."

What a lie. I had stitches and a cast and my arm was strapped against my body by a kind of modified straitjacket. It hurt like hell. It felt like something was eating it.

"I'm sorry I yelled," Mom said.

"It's OK," I said. "Me too."

We were back on the highway proper. We crossed the railroad tracks and passed the Wal-Mart. The rain had slacked up.

"I know you're disappointed, Travis," Mom said. "I just want you to be realistic. Accept that you're injured. It won't be forever."

"I hope not."

"It won't. You'll heal. Trust me."

She pitched her cigarette out of the car.

"You ought to quit those," I said.

"I ought to haven't ever started them in the first place. I never smoked until your daddy's accident but I don't think I've missed a day since. Travis, listen to me. You're at a stage of your life where you'll think you're treading water and aren't making any progress more often than not. Don't worry. You're making plenty of progress every day because time really is passing. God. It flies so fast when you're in high school. It doesn't seem to but it does. These next couple of years will be over before you know it and then you'll wonder where they went. Believe me."

"I believe you," I said.

But I didn't. I felt out of time. I felt like I was stranded in limbo.

"Can you catch a ride home?" Mom said.

I nodded.

"I'll drop you off then," she said. "Just promise me that you won't let them talk you into doing something you can't do."

"Mom."

"I'm serious, Travis. I know how football coaches operate. They'll have you out there if there's any way at all."

"And I'll be out there if there's any way at all."

"I know it. That's what bothers me."

"Give me a break, Mom."

"Be reasonable, Travis. You're too young to get yourself permanently damaged just because of football. It's just not worth it."

I couldn't have disagreed with her more. At that point football was the reason I got up in the morning. It was worth whatever I had to give to be able to play it including, I thought, the risk of a permanent injury. That's how naive I was. I didn't realize that if I had been allowed to play and had seriously injured myself, I would have forfeited playing ball in the future. But the future didn't exist for me then. All I could see was the not-too-bright present.

It was drizzling when we got to Roughneck Field but the sky didn't look dark or heavy enough for an all-out storm of the kind that would keep the team indoors for practice. Crews's pickup and Wroten's station wagon were parked out front. It was fifth hour, their prep period. I promised Mom that I'd be reasonable and told her that I'd see her later. She hugged me before I got out of the car. It embarrassed me because I was afraid that Crews or Wroten might see, which was ridiculous. Being sixteen isn't the easiest thing I've ever done. It's the year of your life when you want your mother to hold you tighter than she ever has and let you go for good at the same time. You're confused. You love her and you know that she loves you, but you're sixteen years old and it makes you uncomfortable when you have to demonstrate it in a place where somebody else might see. You don't want to be a mama's boy. You do but you don't. You're ready for the love that exists between the two of you to be understood and not displayed, especially in public where it might be seen as a sign of weakness.

I watched Mom drive toward the first curve in the road that goes around the stadium. I kept my eyes on the car until I couldn't see it anymore. My elbow was aching inside and out. It was bad enough when I was lying down or sitting, but I'd learned in the hospital that when I was standing a surge of blood would rush to the injury, which made it throb like it was going to explode. On top of that the way my arm was rigged against my body threw my equilibrium off. I had a different center of balance. I walked leaning slightly to the right because I felt like I was falling down if I didn't.

I moved through the dressing room and noticed that my locker didn't have a practice uniform in it. My pads, my shoes, and my hat were there but no jersey or pants. Cody the Gimp. Everybody else's gear was ready to go. I tried not to think about it.

The coaches were in their office across from the concession stand beneath the home side. They were in there breaking down a video. I stood outside the door and listened. They'd watch a play, talk about it, run it back, and watch it again. I didn't want to interrupt them but I didn't have any choice. I waited for a pause, then I knocked.

"It's open," Crews said.

The only light in the office came from the big-screen TV, Farmerville against Cotton Valley from the week before. Farmerville was Oil Camp's next opponent. Crews was sitting in a folding chair directly in front of the TV. He was holding the remote control. His back was to me. Wroten sat at a student's desk against the right wall. He was diagramming the play they'd been watching. I left my hand on the knob when I pulled the door to.

"What if we shot a linebacker through there?" Wroten said. "Looks to me like they're begging for it."

"Let's see," Crews said.

He thumbed the Play button and the figures on the TV screen came to life. Farmerville had the ball and was running a sprint-out pass. The guard to the action side pulled to protect the quarterback. Crews paused it.

"What's the tendency on this?" he said.

"They always and I mean without fail show it to the strong side," Wroten said. "We could just read that guard."

"We'll read him and shoot from the back side if he pulls," Crews said. "That'll fly. Get that light, Cody."

I still don't know how he knew that I was the one who'd come in. I hadn't seen him look away from the screen. I flipped the light switch and swallowed hard.

"Coach," I said.

"How's it feel?" Crews said.

"Not great," I said.

"Have a seat," Crews said.

He indicated another folding chair. It was propped against the wall to my left. I did my best to unfold it and sit down without looking too spastic. Neither coach made a move to help me but both of them were watching me close. I could feel their eyes.

"What's on your mind?" Crews said.

Without taking his eyes off of me, he laid the remote control on top of the TV. Then he crossed his legs, laced his fingers together, and held his knee with both hands.

"Well?" he said.

"I need one play to letter," I said. "I'd really like to get it if I can. I'll do anything you want me to."

I knew immediately that I'd made a mistake. Crews studied me until I squirmed.

"Can you catch a snap to punt?" Wroten said.

"I don't know," I said.

"Even if you could, what would you do if the runner broke free and you had to make the stop?" Crews said.

"I'd try to make it," I said.

"Here," Wroten said.

He reached down beside his desk, picked up a football, and lobbed it to me. It was a soft pass but I wasn't ready for it. I tried to hook the ball with my good arm. I had it for a second but it got away from me. It hit the floor and bounced. I stopped it with my foot. I felt humiliated. I didn't even ask for another chance. The point had been made.

"I appreciate your problem, Cody, but frankly speaking I'm a little disappointed in you, son," Crews said. "What you're asking for is as selfish a thing as I've ever heard. You've put yourself ahead of the team. What if we did let you get your play and something went wrong? What if there was a breakdown at your position because you weren't able to go full speed? Where would we be then?"

I looked at Wroten. His face was as neutral as the wall behind him. He seemed bored.

"I hadn't thought of it that way," I said.

Crews uncrossed his legs and leaned toward me.

"Obviously not. You only thought of yourself, which is understandable up to a point. But others are involved here. It's not just you. There's no place for selfishness on the football field. We have to put the best eleven people we've got out there. If somebody's injured he can't help us so we can't line him up just to get his dadgum letter. This is a team game, son. Is that understood?"

His face had turned redder and redder as he spoke.

"Yessir," I said.

"I hope so."

I stood. The pain in my arm made my head spin. I walked to the door and reached for the knob. Then I turned around. I was going to say something to cover my mistake, something to let him know that even though I was out I wanted to contribute somehow. I could help Grease and Lyndon with their chores during the week. I could run balls in and out during the games. I could do any of a number of things. But Crews cut me off before I could speak.

"Hit that light on your way out," he said.

The glove was on the ground. The next move was mine and I wouldn't have a chance to make it until Spring Ball.

I did lend Grease and Lyndon as much of a hand as I could for a few days, but they had a certain way of doing things so I mostly just slowed them down. Once I quit doing that I was strictly an observer. I was nothing more than a Rattlesnake, which is what we call guys who don't go out for sports, play in the band, or join clubs. They're just sort of there taking up space. They slither around in your peripheral vision, uninvolved. I thought about becoming one for real. I seriously considered it. I even tried to hang around with a few of them but we had nothing in common so that didn't last long. The only thing any of them seemed to halfway care about was whose turn it was to be responsible for getting their weekend liquor. Rattlesnakes live in a closed world. They aren't interested in proving themselves to other people, which is fine. It's actually kind of admirable in a weird way. I'm just not built like that at all. I'm built so that when a glove is on the ground I have to deal with it. I have to prove myself.

I ended up dressing out for the Pineview game. It was only a formality though, a way of keeping myself from going crazy. My elbow was mending without complications but Dr. Wilcox refused to take a chance on letting me practice or play. I was only technically on the team. All I could do was go through pregame cals, stand with the subs during Team Offense and Team Defense, then watch from the sideline in a spotless uniform, which was actually more frustrating than watching from the sideline in street clothes. Either way I wasn't going to be a three-year letterman after all.

Oil Camp won and entered the playoffs with a 7–3 record, upset Lake Providence on the road in the first round, then got crushed at home by Opelousas Catholic. I was disappointed but I didn't go into deep mourning over it. To me losing to the Academy of the Immaculate Conception coonasses just meant that an absurd season was over and done with. It was a relief. I couldn't wait for April and Spring Ball. I couldn't wait to pick up that glove and start trying to make Crews forget that I'd asked him for something I shouldn't have.

Football is like most things. The best part is looking forward to it. Sometimes you only think you know what it is that you're looking forward to. I had no idea how hard that spring was going to be.

I started running the day after the Opelousas Catholic game, the Saturday after the season ended. I ran on the field and I ran in the stands. Back and forth, up and down. I ran and ran. Even when I worked on my punting I ran. I covered my kicks. I watched the ball hit, roll, and stop, then I sprinted to it. Again and again. I ran to school, I ran to the station, and I ran home. I had Dr. Wilcox's go-ahead to lift when we opened Fourth Quarter weight training in February but I kept running. I lifted and ran, lifted and ran. I never stopped running. I ran through the winter. I ran all the way to Spring Ball. I was looking for that glove. I found it and I picked it up. My name was listed second on the depth chart.

"You want to be a Roughneck, Cody?"

"Yessir."

"How bad, Cody? How bad do you want to be a part of this football team?"

"Bad."

"Prove it then. I want you here and I want everybody else over there. Cody says he wants to be a Roughneck, men. Let's find out. This is Blood Alley. Let's find out if Cody really wants to be a Roughneck."

He dragged four blocking dummies into the end zone and made a narrow corridor with them, two on each side. Lunk and I lined up. Crews blew his whistle. Lunk and I collided. Halliburton and I lined up. Crews blew his whistle. Halliburton and I collided. One by one they took their places across from me. We lined up. Crews blew his whistle. We collided. Over and over. Line up. Hear the whistle. Collide. Blood Alley. Every afternoon.

For the first time ever I didn't enjoy hitting. It wasn't fun. It was merely painful and the pain got worse every day. By the end of the second week the water in the bowl was turning pink instead of yellow whenever I peed. Seeing it scared me and I began to hear a voice telling me to quit. I thought about checking my gear in but I'd had a taste of life as a Rattlesnake and that was no good. My only alternative was to stay. Crews must have suspected that. Otherwise he wouldn't have spent so much time trying to kill me, trying to make me better than I am.

"You want to be a Roughneck, Cody?"

"Yessir."

"This is Bull in the Ring, men. Cody's the bull."

They formed a circle around me.

Crews called their names one at a time.

I met them when they came.

I clawed.

I scratched.

I did whatever it took.

As a result I began to hear something from Crews other than that question. He only said it every now and then at first, but by the middle of the third week he was saying it on a regular basis.

"That's it, Cody," he said. "Good job, son."

I guess it's either in you or it isn't. You either want to be a football player or you don't. I found out that it was in me. I found out that I wanted to be a football player. Crews stripped me bare. He stood me at the back boundary of my limits and showed me who I am. He made me prove to him and to myself that I could survive anything. I hated his guts for doing it but when it was over and I saw my name listed among the starters on the final chart I realized that I would have done it for twenty more days if I'd needed to. I'd have done it for twenty weeks, twenty months, twenty years. I was that willing. Crews could have spent the rest of his life trying to run me off and I'd have been out there the day after his funeral lining up, listening for his whistle, and preparing to collide.

The truth of the matter is that everything I've done on the football field from the opening day of Spring Ball last April to Bataan last summer, everything from the Pineland Jamboree in September to yesterday's walk-through, was an attempt to impress Crews. In that way I guess I'm no different from anybody who has ever put on one of these jerseys. We want to do well for Crews because he's the reason Oil Camp has been so successful during the past two and a half decades. There's no other explanation for it. The tradition was in place but losing seasons did happen once in a while until he arrived. He put an immediate end to that by going 6–4 in his first year, which was his worst record and one of only three or four times a team of his failed to reach the playoffs.

So you grow up here dreaming about playing football and when you finally get to, the man you do it for has your complete respect because you know that J. C. Crews *is* Oil Camp football. He's the constant. You may hate and resent him at times and you may want to quit him but you always respect him. Last summer I saw Glen, who'd been out of high school for four years, take a pack of cigarettes from his shirt pocket and hide them in his jeans before going up to talk to Crews.

"No way I'd let that man see me with a pack of smokes," Glen said.

I knew exactly why.

Being a coach must be a lot like being a father. The difference is that no father has as many sons as a coach does. A coach has hundreds of sons but he can't afford to let himself get too close to any of them. He has to treat them all the same because his job is to mold them into a squad. Nobody's special, regardless of his circumstances. When you're in the middle of it, this isn't always easy to understand or deal with. But it has to be that way because the team comes first and you either accept this and make the necessary sacrifice or you get out. There's no in-between. I learned that fact the hard way last spring and I chose to accept it. Crews taught me what it takes to be one of his boys. It takes literally everything you have. Once you've given that and given it unselfishly you're in. You're a Roughneck.

Last spring I found out just exactly how difficult and brutal a task that can be on a physical level and I questioned whether sticking with it was the right thing to do. During the past four weeks I've found out that it can be just as difficult and just as brutal on a mental level and I've been asking myself the same question: Is it right? Sometimes I've thought it was and sometimes I've thought it wasn't. I seem to have changed my mind about it every five minutes. But even when I was thinking that it wasn't right I always acted like it was, so that must be my real answer.

Some of the guys have started to come into the cafeteria for our pregame meal. I watch them for a few minutes, then I stand and stretch my back. I need to start sucking it up and getting myself ready to go do whatever it takes to be a Roughneck one last time.

15

I don't touch my pregame meal. The roast beef looks petrified. The toast looks day-old. The pear and the lettuce look waxen. None of it seems any less appetizing than usual but I'm not hungry so I don't even pick up my fork or sip my tea. I just sit with my arms resting on either side of my tray and watch Lunk across the table. He's shoveling his food in like it's the last he'll ever see. He eats for a while then he drinks some tea. He has three glasses of it and he dumped so much sugar into them that all of it hasn't dissolved. About a quarter of an inch of Imperial Pure Cane has settled like sand on the bottom of each glass. I feel reassured. I'm not eating but Lunk is stuffing himself as always. He's covering me.

Guys have grouped themselves at tables according to friendships. With Lunk and me are Stills, Grease, Beep-Beep, and Halliburton. I've been knowing Lunk, Stills, and Grease since before we had teeth, Beep since kindergarten, and Halliburton since his family moved to Oil Camp from Oklahoma when we were in second grade. We're tight. Nobody's excluded but buds are buds, which is what guys at the other tables would say about who they're sitting with. The only table you wouldn't want to try is the one Crews and Wroten occupy. Being coaches they have that distance to maintain. It's necessary and understood. It's there at all times, presented by them and honored by us.

The discussions that are going on are subdued. It's a rule to keep your voice down during the pregame meal. You're supposed to start getting your mind on the game and keeping your voice down is supposed to help you do it. As if you haven't done it already. As if you haven't been thinking about this week's game almost constantly since you showered after last week's. Sometimes some of the younger guys have a hard time with the volume rule, but as soon as somebody begins to turn it up Crews or Wroten will pull the plug on him. A glance from either one of the coaches will muffle you in a hurry.

The weird thing about all this is that because your mind is already on the game and has been, you don't talk about it directly. Instead you either talk around it or talk about something else to relieve the tension that's building up inside you. I've never heard a word about an upcoming game at a pregame meal and I've never figured out exactly why it is that a little chatter in a normal tone of voice is such a capital offense three and a half hours before kickoff. It seems to me that we'd be better off yelling and throwing food at each other. Nobody's slinging roast beef today though. It sounds like a bunch of murmuring monks in here.

"What're you looking at?" Lunk says.

"A garbage disposal," I say.

"Just getting a little nourishment, T," Lunk says. "I need my strength."

I push my tray toward him.

"Dine away," I say.

"You through?" Lunk says.

"Pretty much," I say.

"Ever try chewing with your mouth closed there, Lunkersan?" Stills says.

"Can't say that I have," Lunk says. He reveals a mouthful.

"Gross," Beep says.

"Pardon hell out of *moi*, Miss Manners," Lunk says.

"You using that pear, Cody?" Halliburton says.

"Go ahead," I say.

Burt stabs my pear with his fork and inserts the whole half into his mouth.

"There's a pear we'll probably be seeing again before the night's over," Grease says.

"I'll let you know if it starts to happen," Halliburton says.

"Speaking of gross, Beep," Lunk says. "I've got one for y'all. True story. Guy at a frat party said he'd bet a hundred bucks he could gross everybody out. This was at Tech. They took him up. He covered their money then he pulled a Baggie out of his pocket and gagged himself till he puked and caught it in the Baggie."

"Pretty gross," Beep says.

"Merely foolish," Halliburton says. "I'd asked for my money back."

"Just wait," Lunk says. "So anyway, this guy carries the puked-in Baggie around with him and shows it to everybody who'll look. They're grossed but not a hundred bucks' worth. Then the band that's playing takes a break. When they leave the stage the guy gets up there and drinks every bit of what's in his bag."

"I'm through," Beep says.

"God almighty, man," Halliburton says. "Who told you that?"

"Can't remember," Lunk says. "I must've read it in the paper."

"You must've made it up is what you must've done," Grease says. "Had to have."

Lunk shakes his head and holds three fingers up like a Boy Scout.

"I can top it," Stills says.

"God, that's gross," Beep says.

"He must've been drunker than anybody ever got," Halliburton says.

"Either that or needed a hundred bucks real bad," I say.

"Probably both," Lunk says.

"I can, y'all," Stills says.

"I don't want to hear another one," Beep says.

"You don't hear this," Stills says. "You see it."

"I can't eat any more either," Halliburton says.

"Wimps," Lunk says.

He continues to chow. The rest of us sit back and cross our legs. We look like one of those commercials where a group of guys are hanging out. They're relaxing and having a nonsense conversation while the camera jumps around the room and every so often zooms in on a jeans tag. We're not really relaxed though. We're just trying to act like it. It's fifteen after four and the jitters are hovering.

"You plan on this week or next, Stills?" Lunk says.

"What say, Beeper?" Stills says.

"Floor's yours," Beep says. "I can handle it."

Stills takes his billfold from his back pocket. He slides a picture out of the plastic photo file.

"This is guaranteed to be the grossest thing you'll ever see," he says.

He lays the picture on the table. It's Lunk grinning big in last year's school shot.

"Stills, you have a point," Halliburton says.

Grease and Beep cover their eyes. I grab my throat.

"Arf-arf," Lunk says.

For a moment it's like we've forgotten what we're about to do. Then everybody remembers again and we all sort of stare at nothing. Stills slowly nods his head. The rest of us have turned into mannequins. This seems to last for a long time but it's probably not even a minute. I'm the first to return from wherever we've been.

"Well, y'all?" I say.

"Let's road," Grease says.

Lunk finishes off his third glass of tea, then all six of us rise and carry our trays to the window. I look over my shoulder as I'm walking toward the door. We've started an exodus. There's a bottleneck of guys in black-and-gold jerseys waiting to set their trays on the conveyor belt that will transport them to the dishwashers.

I ride with Grease in the Corvair because I gave Glen the keys to my bike after the pep rally and asked him to take it home for me. Grease has KOYL tuned in and they're broadcasting a song about sneaking I-Love-Yous on the phone. You can count on KOYL for country and you can count on country for humans who have gotten themselves into some kind of a depressing bind.

"I need a better joke than the one you gave me this morning," I say.

"Let me think," Grease says.

"Don't pull a muscle."

Another song comes on. This one's by a woman singer. She can't get no satisfaction and her tractor won't get no traction. Pitiful. If I tried to hand that line in to Mr. Parke he'd keep me after school for a month. It's a wonder I ever get in the mood for country but sometimes I do. What's really a wonder is that people like Grease stay in the mood for it all the time.

"I can't think," Grease says.

"Neither can I," I say.

I turn the radio down.

"Aw, man," Grease says. "That's a good song."

He turns it back up.

"I'm coming after you if that whiny junk gets stuck in my head," I say.

Grease just sings along.

We're moving through the intersection of Park and Marietta, Nita's street. Roughneck Field is about a mile straight ahead. I can see the red brick of the stadium's west side and the back of the silver sheet-metal press box rising above to mirror the lowering sun. We pass City Pond, the baseball field, the swimming pool, and the tennis courts. When the road flares to become the parking lot, Grease lifts his foot off the accelerator, applies the brakes, and points to what I'm already looking at.

Pineview has arrived. The Pelicans have come to our stadium aboard a Continental Trailways bus with a banner attached to its side.

"What a bunch of total and complete morons," Grease says.

We can read the banner from where we are but Grease wheels us up for a closer look. We cruise the Trailways like a pilot fish cruising a whale. We inspect the banner. It's white with green lettering:

SURRENDER ROUGHNECKS

Grease cuts his eyes toward me. We both shake our heads.

"Can you believe this?" Grease says.

"Tacky," I say.

"Dumb," Grease says. "Very dumb."

So far my only prediction about the game has been that a touchdown will decide it. That hasn't changed but I'm making another one to go with it now. I'm predicting that when people get together tomorrow, next month, and on into the future to talk about the time Oil Camp and Pineview played for State, they'll remember Pineview's Trailways and admit that chartering a bus for a twelve-mile trip would have been a great stunt if it had been left at that but the banner ruined it. The banner, they'll agree, was classless. It was a bad idea and the first real mistake either team made.

"I kind of like it," I say.

"I kind of do too," Grease says. "If it wasn't so stupid I'd go rip it off."

"You still owe me a joke," I say.

"I'm still trying to think of one, home," Grease says. "Keep your zipper up."

EVENING

16

There's a game program in each of our lockers. On the cover is a painting of a receiver and a defender going up for a pass. Both players have their eyes on the ball and both of them are reaching for it. They've left the ground to meet it as it descends and neither one appears to have an advantage. The ball is poised just beyond their outstretched fingers. Which one will come down with it? Maybe the receiver, maybe the defender, maybe neither. You have to decide for yourself how the play will turn out and you don't have anything solid to base your decision on so you could be wrong no matter what. Or right. It's pure speculation. The situation itself is even debatable. The only sure thing is that here are two players going up for a pass. The play and the game it comes from could mean everything or nothing. There are no clues, just the moment and the moment is outside of time. Time doesn't exist anymore. Time has been defeated. Time has stopped and the ball hangs there like all that's possible.

The program is printed on a single sheet of paper

folded once, a rush job for the playoffs. I open it up. The fold halves a picture of a sweaty Coke bottle. The Real Thing. Always. Across the bottom are drawings of all the signals an official might give during a football game. Touchdown, safety, time-out, offsides, clipping, and so on. Above the signals on either side of the fold are the team rosters, us on the left, Pineview on the right. I scan the list of Pelicans. There he is.

53   Jericho Grooms   C/NG   Sr.

I look myself up on the other side. It's always nice to see your name in print unless it's in a paragraph that says you did something you didn't do like miss the ball on a punt.

77   Travis Cody   C/NG   Sr.

I'm glad they didn't include our vital statistics here. Sometimes they do. The program from the November 20 game has them: 6-2, 230 for Grooms and 5-11, 205 for me. On paper it's a mismatch, a mistake, a heavyweight paired against a cruiserweight and I'd just as soon not have to read about it. I can compensate for the difference when we're on defense by playing a couple of feet off the ball, so I'm not really worried about that. I'd actually rather be smaller than my blocker. Turn it around though, and I'm wishing that I weighed fifteen or twenty more pounds. There's no way to compensate when you're on offense against a bigger man. You're stuck and he'll crowd you. Grooms does that well. He gets right in your face. Our hats will almost touch before the snap when I'm on O and he's on D. We're ready to block them in a 4–3 with Jericho at middle linebacker if they show it, but they didn't the other night and I'm not expecting them to tonight. What I'm expecting is a forty-eight-minute war with relief only when I punt. Cody vs. Grooms. Trench City.

It's a little past four-thirty. I won't look at the clock again. I won't have to. I'll try to forget what time it is, but I'll be able to tell it within five minutes by the way I'm feeling. My nerves will count me down to seven-thirty. They'll tick off every second until I'm jangling like an alarm from head to toe. The itinerary is set. Crews types it up and inserts it into our game plan handout every week. It's always the same home or away.

> 4:45 Taping
> 5:30 Last call for taping
> 5:45 Lights-out
> 6:30 Dress for pregame
> 6:40 Pregame
> 7:10 Return to dressing room
> 7:20 Team entrance
> 7:25 Coin toss
> 7:30 Kickoff

Everybody has a ritual that he goes through from now until pregame. I may have discarded most of my nets today but my last few are in place. I can see Mr. Parke shaking his head. Sorry, Mr. P, but I've got to have them now. I'm helpless at this point. I'm like a robot.

I strip, then I put on my jock, my gym shorts, my sweatpants, my half-shirt, my double-cotton, my socks, and my shoes. We're free to go outside and walk the field or sit in the stands until we get taped. I don't like to get taped right away so I always go out and take a leisurely lap or two around the field. I won't talk to anybody unless they ask me a direct question.

I move through the dressing room with my head down. Several guys swat me on the rear. I walk outside. The sun is gone and the air is getting cooler. The stadium is empty. The field is abandoned. I open the gate and jog across the south end zone. The grass is thick and springy. I can smell the dirt beneath it, which reminds me of Mary Helen Clampit's perfume. I turn upfield and high-step to the forty. I cross eight lines of fresh white chalk then I walk. I concentrate on my back. I probably should have had Nita redo my wrap for me but I wanted to leave it off for a while. I'm feeling a little tight again. I stop and stretch. I bend over. Before the November 20 game I could put my palms flat on the ground without any problem. I couldn't do that now to save my life. I'm determined to at least touch the grass though. It hurts but I make myself do it. I stand. I try to remember what it's like to wake up and live a day without being tired and having to carry some kind of pain around. Impossible. During Bataan you develop a body ache that won't leave you for the rest of the season. It's with you in the morning, it's with you in the afternoon, and it's with you in the evening. As the days and weeks go by, it seeps down into your bones and makes you weary. You decorate it with bumps and bruises and scrapes and cuts, and you shoulder the whole heavy load every day. You pick it up and wear it like a badge. You almost get used to it but you never quite do, even though you forget feeling any other way.

I roll my neck and windmill my arms. I move forward. I debate another pool but that would drain me. I'll just have Lyndon rub me down instead. After my ankles are taped I'll have him knead me and karate-chop me and then I'll have him wrap me in new heat. I'll have Dr. L prepare me like so much meat.

I'm in the north end zone. The pumping unit is to my right. The o-wee-wee bows and rises, bows and rises. I look across and see some Pineview guys milling around outside their dressing room. Three of them have on their game pants, white with green stripes. The other two are in green sweats. All five of them are staring at me. My route will take me within a few feet of them. I don't alter it. I lift my chin.

"What's up?" one says.

"Not a lot," I say.

"Y'all ready?" another one says.

His eyes let me know that he doesn't think so. He's the smallest of the five. I figure him for a soph who has been in for maybe half a dozen late plays all season. Even in his saggy sweat suit he looks skinny and frail. He's probably the safety on their scout team. Tonight he'll watch from the sideline. He'll jump back when the action gets too close to him, then he'll spring forward clapping his bony hands and talking all manner of trash. He'll praise the Pelicans and ridicule the Roughnecks. Pineview won't know a more dedicated fan. He'll have as much to say about the game as Okie Colbert and the crew at the fence will.

I nod.

"Y'all?" I say.

"You better believe it, Cody," the smallest one says.

I'm surprised that he knows who I am. I can't stop myself from smiling at him.

"Later on then," I say.

"Yeah," he says. "Later on the Camp dies."

Feisty little bastard. I don't reply. Still smiling I high-step from the ten to the fifty. I suck cool air deep into my lungs. I ease into a slow jog and circle the field one more time. When I get back to the gate I glance at the darkening sky. A few stars are already visible in the east. It's going to be a beautiful night, clear and cool and perfect for a football game.

Grease is busy laying out thin mattresses on the dressing-room floor. He drops one in front of my locker.

"Got you a joke," he says. "Ready?"

"Fire away," I say.

"OK. Why do guys from Pineview wear rubbers on their ears?"

I shrug.

"Because they don't want to get hearing aids."

"Woof-woof," I say. "Get out of town, Grease."

I feel the same way about puns that I do about country music. Sometimes I like them; sometimes I don't. Mostly I don't. I'm not good at them either. I can't even remember the last time I came up with one. Hearing aids. I guess I've heard worse.

I sit down in my locker. I take off my shoes, my

socks, and my sweatpants. I stand and go to the training room. I grab a razor and a can of Foamy. In the shower I shave my legs from midcalf down. I've tried Nair but it smells awful and it takes too long. Shaving is more immediate and the result is better anyway. It leaves your skin as smooth as sanded wood. I return the blade and the cream. Crews is available. I hop up on one of the padded tables and scoot myself against the wall.

"How is it?" Crews says.

"A little tight but I'm OK," I say.

"You have plenty of time for a whirlpool," Crews says.

"I think I'll be better off if I stay out."

"It's up to you."

"A rub and a wrap ought to be enough."

"Fine," Crews says. "Whatever you think."

He goes to work on my left ankle. He dries it, then he puts a prewrap on it. He pushes my toes back with his chest. He takes all the slack out of the joint. He'll leave some in the right one for punting but he's going to make the left one nearly immobile. I watch him start a roll of tape and do a figure eight across the top of my foot and back around under my heel. He's wearing a plain black T-shirt. His arms are long and muscular and he handles the roll with quick, expert movements. He unwinds, tears, and applies the white adhesive in a smooth rhythm. Watching him I feel a wave of goose bumps spread on my neck and splash up the back of my head. I close my eyes.

"There'll be some scouts here tonight," Crews says.

I manage not to open my eyes.

"Where from?" I say.

"All over. The press box is filled so we're going to have to put a few of them in the bleachers."

He starts on my right ankle.

"Ever heard of Dexter Tinsley?" he says.

My eyes are open before I can stop them. Crews knows. He knows everything. How could I possibly have been stupid enough to think that Tinsley or anybody else would scout a player without telling his coach?

"He called me last weekend. Said there was a kid of mine he'd noticed on tape and asked me if I thought it would be worth his while to take a closer look."

A surge of adrenaline floods my system.

"What'd you tell him?"

"See if I've left you anything in that right one," Crews says. "It may be too tight."

I get down from the table and lift myself on tiptoes three or four times.

"Just right," I say.

I raise my eyes to meet Crews's. I want to ask him what he told Coach Tinsley again but I make myself stay quiet. My heart feels like it's climbing up into my neck. Crews holds my gaze for a long time. It's like we're playing chicken with our eyes. Crews is winning. I'm about to bail but just before I do he softens his look enough to keep me in place.

"I told Tinsley the truth, son. I told him the kid he was talking about would make his team if he got the chance to because he's not a quitter. Go get your heat wrap on."

He turns away.

"Coach?"

Crews faces me again.

"Thanks a lot."

Crews nods. That's all. He's not letting me get any closer to him. Maybe he will after the game. We'll have a new and different relationship then. I won't be one of his boys anymore, just somebody who used to be and who is a better person because of it.

I take off my double-cotton and half-shirt. I stretch out on Lyndon's table.

"All yours, medicine man," I say.

Lyndon works me over. His hands aren't magic like Nita's but they'll do. Anybody's would do right now because I'm so elated that I'm feeling no pain. I'm almost giddy, which is the last thing I need to be. I need to be steeling myself. I need to be putting my face on but all I can think about is that Crews just officially sanctioned me as a football player. I feel older somehow, older and more capable. I feel initiated. It's like I've finally crossed the line that separates desire from achievement.

"Loose?" Lyndon says.

"As ten geese."

I sit up. Lyndon cuts a square from a Pampers. He spreads Atomic Balm on it with a tongue depressor.

"Here," he says. "Put this where you want it. What're you grinning so big about?"

"It's personal," I say.

"Must be that Tyler girl. You're whipped, Cody. Bad whipped."

I let him think what he wants. I press the gooey plastic against my back with both hands. The balm is hot on my skin. I hold my arms up while Lyndon wraps me with an extralong Ace bandage that goes from my waist to my chest like a corset. When he's done I put my shirts back on and ask him for a roll of tape. He places one in my hand.

"Much obliged," I say.

At my locker I slip my knee and thigh pads into my pants, run my belt through the loops and the slits Grease cut into my towel, snap my hip and butt pads onto the belt, step into the left leg then the right leg, and yank the whole rig up. I leave the fly laces and the belt undone. I do a couple of deep knee bends. The pants are black with two thin gold stripes on the side of each leg, the hip and butt pads and the belt are gold, and the towel is white. The gear feels as snug as a second skin. I sit down and put my black leggings on. I tape them just below my knees, then I pull on my white tube socks. I'm moving as if I'm in a trance.

I look around the room. Most of the other guys have begun to go deep inside of themselves too. We're starting to search for what it is that makes us who we are. When we find it we'll offer it in exchange for our places on the team. One by one we'll transfer our identities to the larger thing until everybody is outside of himself. Then, united, we'll draw ourselves back for the final and most important shot that we'll ever take together.

I think of the bet Mr. Shackleford said you could get on the game and wish that all the jokers who gave us and five points away could come in here right now and see some of these faces. They'd probably just go ahead and write out their checks.

17

Lights-out. Al Green is on the box low. Al and those horns are serenading us. I'm on a mattress near the radiator. I listen to Al sing while the radiator clunks, hisses, and ticks. Occasionally I hear footsteps in the bleachers above us. I close my eyes and breathe in the smell of the dressing room. I think about my daddy and my brother and all the guys who have passed through here over the years. I think about those kids out on the playground this afternoon. Some of them will be Roughnecks in a few years. They'll carry on the tradition. They won't watch us tonight though. They're too young. They're too busy dreaming their dreams. Tonight they'll be in the clearing behind the scoreboard end zone playing their own game, using a wadded-up Coke cup for a ball the way me, Lunk, Stills, Beep-Beep, Halliburton, and even Grease and Lyndon did when we were their age. Playing pretend football in that clearing with a paper-cup ball seems as close to me as this morning.

I can't believe how fast today has passed. It's like

I was just waking up and "Hey Tonight" was playing on the radio. I've been awake since five-thirty. I ought to be wiped out but I'm not. I'm too nervous and excited to be wiped out. I'm lying here on my back with my hands behind my head and my right leg levered over my left knee. My foot is chopping the air like an ax. The jitters are starting to swoop. I'm not feeling quite as capable as I was a while ago. My hands are clammy and my throat is dry. This is good though. This is the way I should be feeling. You'd have to be dead not to feel some terror less than ninety minutes before a game.

Somebody is throwing up in one of the stalls. I wonder if it's Halliburton getting rid of that pear. If it is I wonder if he told the Greaser. Burt has a big job ahead of him too. Ramsey Godchaux. But Ramsey Godchaux isn't Jericho Grooms. I've drawn the beast. We'll go man-to-man for the second time. He has a district title to show for the first meeting but that's just a ridge. The mountain is what we're after tonight.

Grooms will only play defense in college, probably outside linebacker. He's too small to be a college center so they'll move him across, stand him up, and place him at the turn. Some people wonder why Webb doesn't use him at linebacker on every defensive down. They think he's wasted at nose. They're wrong. Webb has two wicked linebackers and he likes Grooms up front because he's so swift off the ball. He wrecks the middle. Even though I've watched it too many times to count, I still haven't figured out how he got under me on the conversion. It was the only play he made in our backfield that night. I made three in theirs but his one counted. My three were nothing but stats. His one was the difference and he wouldn't have made it if he'd been at linebacker.

The jitters wash over me in a hot wave. I'm slick with sudden sweat and my gut is fluttering. Think of something else. Think of Nita. Picture her. Picture her fine dark eyes. Picture the delicate line of her jawbone. Picture the pleasant curve of her hips. Picture her standing against that pine with her hair still lakewater damp and her tanned face tilted back so that you could look straight into those eyes while she surprised you and maybe herself by saying that she wouldn't mind being your valentine for life. Picture her naked, the final frontier.

The radiator ticks and Al Green sings better than any man ever has. He's deep into "Let's Stay Together," and he's playing around with the words. Sometimes he just holds them out and sometimes he adds extra syllables. His voice is high but it's full. It's more like an instrument than something human and the message it's delivering goes well with the picture of Nita that's in my head.

The beating of footsteps above us is getting more and more persistent. Horns are honking in the parking lot. It's full dark outside by now and the crowd has begun to assemble. The field lamps are on. Once when we were about to run through the hoop Stills said, "Look at the theater, y'all. Now ain't that something to see?" The theater. Green grass lined every five yards and bordered by clean white chalk under strong lamps on tall stanchions. What a sight. What a pretty thing to see.

Tonight will be my last time to see it as a player if I don't get that scholarship. I can't imagine life without games to play, without all the waiting and wondering and doubting that you go through before them, without the buildup of tension and the release of it when you finally enter the theater to find out what you can and can't do one more time. I'd miss it. I'd probably even miss practicing.

It's like Lunk said one time: "Football is the worst game to practice for but, man, it's the best one there ever was to play."

He was exactly right. Practice is pure hell on everybody concerned and anybody who claims to enjoy it is either crazy or lying because it's not football any more than going to the grocery store is cooking. It prepares you for the real thing and you suffer through it because being prepared is necessary and it lets you answer some questions: Can you bear it? Do you have the guts, the determination, and the will to play? Is what you're being asked to do worth the effort? Those are the easy ones, of course, the ones everybody who puts on a hat and goes out there tonight finally had to have said "Yessir" to. Otherwise he'd be riding around with a bunch of Rattlesnakes drinking beer and laughing at all the stupid jocks. The other question practice raises is a little harder, a little closer to the bone: Why are you doing this and not something else?

Lying here I realize that for me the answer has two parts. First, I love having earned my place on the team and with it the right to stand with and compete against a group of guys who have done the same thing. Second, I honestly do love the game. I love it and I believe in it, which is something that I always seem to come back around to during the last little bit before we pad up and head for the theater. No matter what has happened I always seem to make that circle.

Scholarship or not, I'll have to give up the game sooner or later. It doesn't necessarily have to be sooner though. It could be later, much later. Maybe I've known all along without being able to see it until just now what it is that I should do with myself in the future. I can almost picture myself on a practice field somewhere. I'm wearing a sweat suit and a bill cap, and I'm surrounded by sweaty teenagers who hate my guts for trying to make them better than they are. I lift my whistle and blow it. I shake my head.

"Line that up again, offense."

"Yessir."

"We need a better view here, scouts. Some of y'all look like you're walking around in a dadgum museum. But I guess that's understandable considering that our so-called offense seems to have turned into a bunch of statues."

"Yessir."

"Can we get nuts for a change? I mean, does anybody mind if we make this one live?"

"Nosir!"

"I didn't think so. All right, scouts. You know what's coming. Let's see you stop it."

"Yessir!"

"Offense, y'all had better not let these people stop you."

"Yessir!"

"Do you want to be a Whatever?"

"Yessir!"

"How bad, men? How bad do you want it?"

"Bad, sir."

"Prove it."

Then they collide. They give me everything they have. They show me what they've got—partly out of hatred, partly out of fear, and partly out of respect. And when it's done I blow my whistle again.

"That's it, men. Good job."

I'm smiling when I say it but only on the inside. I don't want anybody to think that I'm completely satisfied because if I do they might let up. They might coast. They might get the idea that football is a forgiving game, which I know it most definitely is not.

Excellent. Very smooth. I'm totally losing my perspective here. I'm doing exactly what Pawpaw did and what Mrs. Hammontree does except I'm doing it in the opposite direction. I'm drifting into the future and getting completely out of touch with reality. Grooms is probably down at the other end banging his head against the wall. He's probably totally psyched for the issue at hand, the *now.* He'll be out there. He and all the rest of the green hats of Pineview will be out there wanting what we want no less than we do. They've paid the same price we've paid and they've come to collect the same receipt but the receipt can't be divided.

Concentrate.

Offense. I have to block him away from every play when we have the ball. I have to engage and drive. I have to force him back and create a hole.

Defense. I have to shed him and find the play when they have the ball. I have to engage and slide. I have to read the flow and disappear.

Control him. Make him watch the clock. Scratch and claw. Do what it takes. Don't quit. Never quit. No matter what. Do not surrender to him or to your pain. Fight him all the way down every time. Hand him his jock on a plate.

Grooms. I know that he'll get his licks in, as Webb put it, and I know that it'll be nobody's fault but mine when he does. I just want to keep those licks to a minimum, starting with our opening play. If I can pancake him right, then I'll have him on even terms. I'll finally be all the way out from under the shadow that's been hanging over me since November 20. I'll feel like I'm in charge of my immediate destiny and that's what I need more than anything else. I need to believe, to really believe.

. . . he's not a quitter.

I repeat the words like I'm casting a spell but they don't help. I'm too buzzed. My nerves are peeled. It's almost time. I can feel it. The clock is in motion. Think positive. Conquer and prevail. There can be no more doubts.

I crawl to my locker. I find my way to it in the dark. I fish around and locate my jeans. I dig the vial from my pocket, open it, and pop three butterfly tablets. Chewing I sit down and reach behind me for my shoes. I slide my feet into them, yank the laces tight, and double-tie them. I secure them with a round of tape, swallow the paste that's in my mouth, and stand.

I take down my shoulder pads. I hold them in my hands until the lights come blindingly on.

"Pad up, Roughnecks," Crews says.

We dress quietly. Lunk pulls my jersey over my shoulder pads. Before I return the favor I read his T-shirt. FOOTBALL IS LIFE. We touch knuckles. I tuck my jersey in. I tie my fly laces and loop the end of my belt through its buckle. I do three deep knee-bends. I look at my hat. It's shiny black with a gold face mask and no trim except for the smudges of color and the dents I've accumulated from head-ons dating back to the first day of full gear during Bataan. There's a long green smear on the left side. I grab the hat by the face mask and put it on. Leaving the chin strap and mouth-piece dangling, I go around the room for fist-fives and eye contact with my teammates. My stomach is churning. It's not fooled by the fake medicine I just ate. I rinse my mouth with cold water from the fountain. I swish it around and spit it into the drain. It hurts my teeth.

Grease wheels the chalkboard out of the training room. Crews stands beside it. Wroten is over by the door. Both coaches are wearing gold sweatshirts with *Oil Camp Football* sewn in black cursive script at chest level. Crews's head is bare. Wroten has on a black bill cap with a gold derrick on its crown.

"Listen up, men," Crews says.

He tosses a piece of chalk from hand to hand. We give him our attention.

"Go slow and easy with your cals," he says. "Take your time. Get good and loose."

He turns, writes two sevens on the board, and circles them. Stills's prediction at the Chowline was right. I'll join him and Lunk as our third captain tonight. We elected them unanimously after a week of Bataan. Crews and Wroten choose an honorary third during lights-out before every game and Crews reveals the choice by writing a number on the board before we go out for pregame. This is the first time he's ever written mine. Somebody whacks the back of my hat. I feel like I'm going to vomit. My mouth begins to gush saliva faster than I can swallow it. I look at the floor. I dry-heave once but that's all. The nausea passes.

"Captains in front," Crews says. "Slow and easy now. All right. Let's go."

Wroten opens the door. He hits me on the shoulder as I follow Lunk and Stills into the night.

"Congratulations, cap," Wroten says.

Another first. I'm too amazed to speak.

The rest of the team falls in behind Lunk, Stills, and me. We slap our thigh pads and clap our hands. We get a rhythm going as we walk toward the gate. *Thump-thump, clap-clap.* I breathe deeply of the cool sweet air. We jog onto the field. Our band jumps into the Olympic TV theme and our fans rattle the gravel in their cans. This is one of two entrances we'll make and the stands are only about half-full so the greeting is reserved. Pineview is at the other end, already into push-ups.

Lunk, Stills, and I face the squad from the

thirty-five yard line. *Thump-thump, clap-clap.* I break the rhythm to fasten my chin strap and adjust the cuffs of my double-cotton. Like an idiot I forgot to tape them. I like them taped at my wrists. *Thump-thump, clap-clap.* When everybody is lined up Stills quits slapping his thigh pads and starts clapping his hands faster and faster. We join him and clap that way until the beat begins to scatter. I glance toward the section of bleachers where the band is sitting and find Nita. She has my jacket with its single letter slash on over her majorette uniform. Her hair is up. You can tell that she's a knockout even from this far away. She blows me a kiss. There's still enough slack in the tension that's gripping me to let me jerk my head back as if the blown kiss has struck me. Nita smiles and mouths three words. I think: *Me too.*

Stills directs us into a set of side straddle hops. We count them off with letters, our voices blending together as one. R-O-U-G-H-N-E-C-K-S, ten of them followed by one-two way-back and windmill toe touches, out behind the barn groin stretches, push-ups, sit-ups, neck bridges, then ten more hops. Crews and Wroten wander among us like farmers inspecting rows of crops. Because I've always been with the body of the team I've never had my back to the opposing players during pregame cals. I can hear Pineview begin and end their exercises. Sometimes their counting mixes with ours. I want to turn around and check them out but I don't. I keep my eyes on the twenty-nine black hats spread out like mutant flowers between me and the south end zone. They reflect the glare of the field lamps.

After cals the linemen go to one side of the field

with Crews and the backs and ends go to the other with Wroten. We line up in two parallel files. Lunk and I are in front at the goal line. Crews stands at the ten.

"First sound, men," he says.

Lunk and I take three-point stances.

"Hut!"

We sprint past Crews. Halliburton steps up to the chalk with Modisette. They take their stances.

"Hut!"

Halliburton and Modisette fire out and sprint the ten yards. When everybody has gone to the ten and back twice the lines turn to face each other. Crews sets himself up between us a step back. My line will be runners. The other guys will hit us but won't take us down. After that we'll switch.

"Good form now, tacklers," Crews says. "Just meet and wrap up. Second sound. Hut! Hut!"

Lunk sticks me, locks his arms, and lets go.

"Somebody block that dude," I say.

Lunk howls like a wolf.

I'm beginning to breathe harder now. I'm settling into the comfortable pace of pregame, the routine of it. We collide without malice at three-quarter speed, form tackling and then blocking: one-on-one, two-on-one, three-on-one. The stands are filling and some of the fence birds have taken their places at the rail. They sip whiskey from their Go-Cups and draw smoke from their cigarettes. I keep my eyes away from Pineview but I'm aware of their movements as flashes of white in the distance.

"Get you some punts, Cody," Crews says.

I motion to Blake Tabor, my backup and our deep

snapper. I trot to the goalpost and Tabor moves to the five, where Grease has set some balls out for me to kick. I'll hit ten from the back of the end zone, then we'll go to midfield.

Wroten sees Tabor and me and waves Beep, Duhon, Beene, and a couple of others out to catch my punts. I lick my fingers and check for wind, an old habit. What little there is comes from the north. It's against me but it's slight. It's nothing to worry about.

Tabor hikes the first ball over my head.

"Easy, Blake," I say. "I'm right here."

Tabor's a soph. He's a good snapper but he has the fears. I retrieve the ball. The hoop we'll run through in a few minutes is leaning against the fence. It faces away from me. I underhand the ball to Tabor.

"That never happened," I say. "OK?"

"OK," Tabor says. "Sorry."

The next snap is low and slow. I scoop it up. Step. Drop. Kick. I know that the result is pretty because of the way the ball felt when it met my foot. I don't need to look.

Tabor improves a little each time and finally sends one back hard and waist high.

"There you go," I say. "That's number seven. Let's frame it."

He puts the next three right where I want them and we head for the fifty. I take a quick look at the Pelicans. They're running plays from the twenty. All I can see is the wall of subs shielding their offense and scout team. Good. They're out of the way. Sometimes Tabor and I get into a traffic jam with the opposing punters or return men when we move to midfield. It's a distraction nobody needs at that point.

We pass the backs going the other way.

"Good boots, Cody," Beep says. "You're killing them tonight, man."

"Credit the hiker," I say.

Grease runs past us with a load of footballs cradled in his arms like firewood. He places them at the fifty and starts away.

"Hey, Grease," I say.

Grease stops. I hold my arms out.

"I need some tape on these," I say.

Grease takes a roll from his utility belt and fixes the cuffs of my double-cotton.

"I like the M&M's one better," I say.

"No problem," Grease says.

I don't think he even heard me. I set up behind Tabor and flap my hands like I'm slinging water off of them to loosen the tape a little bit.

"Whenever, Blake," I say.

Tabor grooves me ten bullets and I knock the ball out of sight every time. I admire the flight of the last one. It hangs high in the night, turns over, and drops into Beep's arms like a mini tornado. He bobbles it. He tucks it in. I like that bobble. I like it a lot.

We finish pregame with Team Offense. Ones and Twos alternate against the scouts. We're not supposed to be live but I tell Modisette that I need real hits from him. We've bopped all season and I know he's getting tired of me beating on him but I have to do it one more time so we go at each other full speed. I want it that way. I want the licks serious and Modisette delivers.

"How to be, Matthew," I say. "How to damn be, bro."

I'm loose and good. I've broken an honest sweat. I'm almost ready.

We leave the field. Music is played and cans are rattled. Voices are raised and hands are clapped. I look up at the press box and see the radio station banner.

KOYL 1630 AM
PROUD TO CARRY ROUGHNECK FOOTBALL

Maddox and Dees are up there setting the stage for those who have tuned them in. Van Noate's undoubtedly up there too, along with all the scouts who have come to watch the phenomenal Jericho Grooms and whoever else might play some impressive ball tonight.

I throw up at the dressing-room door. It's so sudden that I just have to laugh. At least I jerk my face mask up and out of the way in time.

18

This is it. Our band is playing the National Anthem. Lunk, Stills, and I are at midfield with Grooms, Godchaux, and the officiating crew. I'm chewing a stick of Juicy Fruit Lyndon gave me to get the sour taste of throwing up out of my mouth. All of us are facing the flag that's being run up the pole beside the scoreboard by a Boy Scout. The other senior Roughnecks are five or six yards behind Lunk, Stills, and me, and the rest of the team is strung out along the west sideline. Pineview is positioned the same way. Captains, seniors, squad.

". . . at the twilight's last gleaming,"

Crews didn't give a long pregame speech. He just told us that he knew we were prepared, that he had a lot of confidence in us, and that he was as proud of us as any team he ever coached. Then he wrote two words under my number on the board. NO SURRENDER. We touched the SACRIFICE sign on the door as we left the dressing room. Our cheerleaders met us at the gate and walked us across the end zone to the south goal-post. Crews, Wroten, Grease, and Lyndon headed down the sideline to our bench. Grease and Lyndon carried an orange Gatorade cooler between them. Several hundred of our fans had formed a corridor for us to run through. Two girls from the pep squad held the hoop at about the forty, where the corridor ended. I was in the middle of the pack. I looked over the black hats in front of me and saw Stills talking to Tiffany Ward like we were waiting to go see a movie or something. Stills is going to flirt if a girl is around no matter what. Finally Tiff nodded at the other cheerleaders and they took off. We ran behind them. They split into two groups of three when they got to the hoop and Stills broke through the paper that covered it. I don't know what it said but I'd bet that it had a drawing of a guy in a black-and-gold hard hat strangling a green pelican on it. The people that flanked us were a blur of color and voices. They reached out to us as we went by them and they shouted words of encouragement. Our band was blowing loud and fast, and the fans in the stands were rattling their cans and hollering. The roar was tremendous. It was like a prolonged explosion. The cheerleaders came together in front of us and escorted us all the way to the sideline.

"And the rockets' red glare..."

We moved to where Crews and Wroten were standing. We went to them like water to a drain and we clogged there leaping and pounding on each other.

Crews had to yell to make himself heard above the din of the crowd. His face was red and the cords of his neck strained against his skin.

"Receive if possible," he said. "If not we'll defend the north goal. Captains out. Seniors follow."

I unsnapped my chin strap and Lunk, Stills, and I held hands as we walked three abreast to meet Grooms and Godchaux.

"Please rise for our National Anthem," the PA announcer said.

"They've screwed this up," Stills said. "They're not supposed to do this until after the damn toss."

He let go of my hand.

"We've got a hitch in the proceedings, fellows," the head referee said. "No problem. No problem."

He removed his bill cap and placed it over his heart. I took off my hat and tucked it under my left arm. The Oil Camp drummers commenced with a buzzing roll. I watched the glint of Nita's flute as she brought it to her lips.

". . . and the home of the brave!"

The crowd erupts. Lunk, Stills, and I step forward to shake the hands of Grooms and Godchaux. Their jerseys and pants are white with green trim and their hats are the reverse of that. The hats have two white stripes down the center and a white *P* on the sides. Grooms is huge. He looks bigger in white than he did in green the other night. The sleeves of his jersey are cut off so that a gray crescent of shoulder pad is visible on each side. His skin is smooth and tight. His biceps are pumped like softballs and his veins stand out like ropes. He has lampblack under his eyes and his hair is cropped close to his head. Mom was wrong. He's not handsome. He's beautiful. We shake. His hand is as wet as mine. Our eyes meet but only briefly.

The head referee shows us a silver dollar. Liberty's profile is heads. An eagle with spread wings is tails.

"White, you're the visiting team so you'll make the call," the referee says. "Which one of you will do the honors?"

"I will," Grooms says.

His voice is deep. He probably sings bass in their school choir.

"Call it in the air," the referee says. "Heads or tails. We'll let it hit the ground and the side that's up will be our winner. Here we go."

He flips the coin.

"Heads," Grooms says.

The silver dollar lands and bounces. It settles. We crane our necks and lean in to see which side is showing.

"It's tails," the referee says.

He picks it up and displays the eagle.

"Black, you have won the toss," he says. "Would you like to kick, receive, defend a goal, or defer until the second half?"

"Give us the football," Stills says.

"Black has elected to receive," the referee says. "White, you'll be kicking off. Which goal would you like to defend?"

Grooms points to the north, toward the pumping unit. The crowd knows what has happened and is reacting. The referee directs Lunk, Stills, and me to turn our backs to the south end zone, then he has Grooms and Godchaux move in front of us. He pats Stills on the shoulder twice and gives the press-box official the signal that we have won the toss and will receive. He steps over to Grooms, pats him on the shoulder, and gives the kickoff signal.

"This is for the Class Double-A State Championship of Louisiana, fellows," he says. "As captains you will represent your teams in any situation that calls for a discussion. I'll let you know your options whenever such a situation arises. Are there any questions?"

There are not. We put our hats on. I snap my chin strap.

"It's a privilege to be on the field with you tonight, fellows," the referee says. "Good luck to you all. Let's have a good clean ball game."

We slap hands with Grooms and Godchaux and run to the sideline. I spit out my gum on the way. Again we surround Crews and Wroten. We bunch as close together as we can.

"This is what we've been working for since August, men," Crews says. "Let's get after us some Pelicans for the next forty-eight minutes."

We howl and whoop. Crews holds his right hand out like he's testing the air from a floor vent. I lay mine on top of it. We make a stack of hands. Those who can't touch it reach in as far as they can. I'm being crushed from the back and both sides. The stack of hands rises and falls three times.

"Roughneck Pride!" we say.

When we break I find Lunk. We clasp hands like

wrestlers and smash hats to clear our heads but mine's crystal. My knees are mushy and my heart is pumping like a piston but my head is in the zone. I'm hyper-conscious. I hear every sound and I see every sight. Inserting my mouthpiece I jog out onto the field and take my position in the middle of the front line for the kickoff. Both bands are playing and the noise of two entire towns come to see their boys play a little football on a cool and clear December evening has risen to a single continuous shriek that shakes my eyes. Every seat in the house is taken and the congregation at the fence is three deep along both sidelines and around into the end zones. There must be close to ten thousand people here. I grip my mouthpiece with my teeth. I watch the Pineview kicker place the ball on the tee, adjust it, stand, look at it, bend, and adjust it some more. I watch him get it exactly the way it must be to satisfy him. I watch him turn away from it, take seven paces, and wheel around. I watch him draw a deep breath to calm himself. His eyes are on the head referee and the head referee has his arm up. They nod at each other and the referee drops his arm. The kicker hops once and approaches the ball. He sends it high and long. I peel back and the shriek of the crowd becomes a flat hum, still audible but distant now. I check Beep-Beep, who's waiting at the goal line. He steps up and catches the ball at the five. I turn. I'm running point in our wedge. I take out the first white suit I see, crab until I'm up-right again, and look for somebody else but whistles sound and I let up. Beep has gone down behind me. He made it to the thirty-one. Not bad but not great. I trot to the twenty-four. I feel completely alive after some game contact.

"Huddle up!" I say.

I lean over, hands on knees. I stretch my back one last time. The Roughnecks convene. I stare at Stills's shoes. They're mummified. No leather or laces show. He puts his hands on my hat.

"No surrender, bros," he says. "This is show time. I want I-right, X open, Inside Belly Right Pass on the third sound. Third sound, y'all. Ready?"

"Break!" we say and clap our hands.

Grooms is standing casually in front of the ball. When I crouch to grasp it he sinks to his knees then rises into a four-point stance. Watching his feet I rotate the ball so that the laces will meet Stills's right-hand fingers. Grooms scoots his right foot slightly back. I'm going to gamble on Big Daddy's advice and play this down as if Jericho will come to my left. I might as well find out now. I feel Stills flip my towel, slap my rear, and place his knuckles against my crotch. I look Grooms in the eye. It's like we're in a vacuum. Our heads are so close together that I can hear his breathing.

"Travis Cody," Grooms says.

"Jericho Grooms," I say.

"Been thinking about you all day long," Grooms says.

"Been thinking about you all day long too," I say.

"Roughnecks down!"

"Ain't pulling for you though," Grooms says.

"Ain't pulling for you either," I say.

"Readyset!"

"Good luck to you anyway, Travis Cody."

"Good luck to you anyway too, Jericho Grooms."

"Hut! Hut-hut!"

I snap the ball and Grooms slants to my left, then realizes his mistake and tries to spin free but I'm already under him. He's mine. My forearm is on his gut and the side of my hat is on his ribs. I make his momentum work for me. I'm driving the big man back and to the left. I'm erasing him from the play. I'm putting Jericho Grooms and every doubt I ever had into the dirt. I feel him yield, lose his balance, and fall. We go down together. I glance at his face long enough to register the surprise in his eyes, then I look upfield. I see that Beep-Beep is wide open and the crazy desire I have to control time flashes through my mind. It comes and goes without lingering, but for one brief moment I think that if I could I'd arrest time right here while I'm on top and Beep-Beep is getting ready to catch a pass that my teammates and I have just allowed Stills to throw. I know better though. I know that time is already turning this into a memory. I roll away from Grooms and stand in one quick motion. I track the flight of the ball. It's coming down. Beep is reaching for it. He's all alone.

This is only the beginning but it's a good beginning. Totally believing in myself for the first time in four weeks I start to run. I run straight toward the long, hard night ahead and whatever lies beyond. Anything is possible, anything at all. There's nothing that can't happen on this field and in this life. I run toward it with all of my might.